# One Cold Coffee

## A Leelanau Mystery

# Robert Underhill

Also by the author:

Strawberry Moon
Providence Times Three
Cathead Bay
Death of the Mystery Novel
Once Dead Long Dead
Suttons Bay
A Desperate Ruse
That Week in June

# One Cold Coffee

## A Leelanau Mystery

# Robert Underhill

If you live in a land of long winters, you don't just appreciate a cloudless, seventy-five degree July day—you absorb it. I was full out absorbing this morning as I coasted my bike down the last quarter-mile into the village of Lake Leelanau. Here I made a right turn at N.J.'s Market, then shifted into my lowest gear for the short uphill finish. These days I rank my bike routes by the "uphill" portions. Coming here to breakfast with my friends was one of the easiest rides and I made it every morning weather permitting. I dismounted in front of the Caballo Bayo Cafe and walked the bike to the side of the old building where there was an outside counter and stools.

The building, sheathed in the narrow clapboards common over a century ago, was one of the first in the village. It began its long and varied life as Foster's Livery Stable. Below the word, "Foster's" on the handsome new sign, the first Foster had painted the picture of a bay horse, that is, a brown horse with a black mane, tail, ear-edges and lower legs. Over the years the business had morphed into a seed store, a general store and a barber shop before settling in finally as a breakfast and lunch restaurant back in the 1940's. While the sign was repainted each time to indicate the new service or commodity being offered, the horse remained

- touched up a bit each time.

In the 1950's a large contingent of Mexican migrant workers came to this area to help harvest the cherry and apple crops, this being the country's leading producer of the tart, pie-type cherry. The Foster in charge in those years opened up a section of wall on one side of the building to form an outside counter through which food could be served to the migrant workers. The crowd of workers evaporated in the 1960's, when the cherry-shaking machine was introduced: one worker and machine could now do the job of a dozen men. The business got an overhaul in 1980, when a modern kitchen was installed. The outside counter and picnic tables remained, however, because they were popular with the ever-growing number of summer tourists, Leelanau being discovered as one of the most beautiful parts of the entire country.

Oh, and "Caballo Bayo"? That's what the Mexican workers had called the place, because it was Spanish for "bay horse" - the horse on the sign. The Foster at that time liked the sound of it (Ca-by-yo By-o). And, so the refurbished old place took on a new name, The Caballo Bayo Cafe.

Part of the ritual of our small group that met each morning was to arrive when the "Bayo" opened at 7:00 a.m. My friends and I were addicted to the good feeling of getting out and about early. The few people you'd meet at that hour seemed like family.

I expected to see Fuss sitting at the first of the six stools. Not there. He was always the first one here taking the same stool each time with old Oscar napping at this feet after the exhausting three-quarter mile walk from home. I climbed onto the second stool from the

2

end. I could hear the whir of an electric mixer coming from the direction of the kitchen. Stretching over the counter, I grabbed the coffee carafe and a cup.

The sun had cleared the hills to the east of the village and like an eager pup anxious to be noticed, shot through the front windows of the cafe energizing the interior pine-paneling to a rich molasses. I stirred some sugar into my coffee enjoying its aroma and the freshness of the morning. The juicer ceased whirring.

"Morning, Jill," I called in that direction.

"Morning, Al," came back. "Don't tell me you beat Fuss."

"Yeah, scary isn't it? What will happen next?"

She came into view carrying a full pitcher of fresh-squeezed orange juice looking like a disheveled ad for Tree Sweet.

"Wanna hit?" she said already pouring a glass.

"Sure, why not." She knew I was a tomato juice man, but the morning was already off to an odd start.

Jill filled another cup with coffee and placed it on the counter where Fuss always sat.

You'd had to know Fuss (Frank) Quarrals to understand why we were coloring the morning with a strangeness hue. His atomic clock punctuality and rigid habits were a wonder to his friends - and a pain in the ass at times. It was so certain that he'd be sitting here, battered old brief-case on the counter in front of him that I kept glancing to the left to be certain he really wasn't there.

I studied Jill as she went about completing her morning routine: filling salt shakers, replenishing napkin holders and wiping fly specks off the dessert display case.

3

She never had a starched look, but this morning she resembled an unmade bed. She hadn't slept much, that was clear. Starting a couple of days back, her boyfriend, Pete, had been scheduled to have a week off from the Great Lakes freighter on which he crewed, but he'd called to say his leave had been canceled. Had he come last night after all?

I pried. "When is Pete due to have leave again?"

"Who the fuck cares?"

I looked down at my glass of orange juice, turning the glass slowly, choosing my words wisely.

"Ahh," I said.

She made a furious pass over the counter with a rag. I looked at my juice and waited.

"Called his cell last night. He didn't pick up. Out on the lake the phone coverage can be spotty, so I called the ship. They have some kind of radio/phone hook-up. The guy who answered thought I was someone else and let it slip that Pete was on leave this week. Left yesterday morning."

She turned abruptly to open the refrigerator and stare into it, but I caught the glistening of tears. She was in pain and I hated to see it.

"Sorry," I said to her tense young back. So she had been up most of the night crying . . . or getting even.

I caught movement out of the corner of my eye and looked around expecting to see a tardy Fuss depositing his long bones on the first stool and started to frame a smart remark to throw in his direction. Instead, it was Sam I was looking at. Big Sam August with his enviable full head of curly silver hair and his beautiful duds. This morning it was a summer-weight, plum car-

4

digan over a gray silk shirt. He exuded that kind of confidence seen in guys who'd long had more money than they could find a way to spend. He was also the kind of guy one couldn't help liking.

"Morning, Sam."

"Morning, Al. Where's Fuss?"

"Beats the hell out of me."

"As I drove by his house on the way here, I noticed that his car wasn't in the driveway as usual. I thought he must have driven here this morning instead of walking."

Both Sam and Fuss had houses on Lake Leelanau. Sam's was two miles from the Bayo, Fuss's less than half that. I waited while he engaged Jill in the banter that was part of securing his first cup of the morning. He was a retired beer distributor from Detroit. When he'd turned the business over to his two nephews, his wife, Natalie, wanted to get him as far away from his old cronies as she could manage – while still having good shopping for herself - maybe New York or Paris. Northern Michigan was the farthest he'd agreed to. This decision, for Natalie, required frequent out of town shopping trips. That was fine with Sam; he played a lot of golf. I kidded him one morning that I'd heard it was the Mafia that ran beer and liquor distribution in Detroit. Sam laughed heartily - but didn't deny it.

I had been a builder in a Detroit suburb – four to six custom homes a year--before I retired eight years ago—before my wife, Mary, died four years later. Her death had come suddenly and unexpectedly leaving me devastated and with a lot to figure out. Like who I was without her – what I should do with my time.  I knew our house in Birmingham was too large for me to live in alone and should be sold. That's about all I knew for sure - sell the house. But then what? Buy a smaller house right there? Both of our children lived in Chicago . . . move there? I needed time to think. We'd owned a small, vacation cottage for years in the northern part of the state. So, I sold the Birmingham house and – just until I got my bearings - moved into the cottage. That was four years ago.

Anyway, I'd been here in the cottage for a couple of lonely months, feeling low and sleeping little, when, as I lay awake one morning staring at my bedroom ceiling, I felt the urgent need to get out of the house – find a place to have breakfast – not one more solitary bowl of cornflakes eaten by myself. I knew of a small restaurant in the nearby village where the family had eaten occasional hamburgers—good hamburgers as I recalled. It was a little after seven and I had doubts about it being open, but I decided to give it a try. Driving up to the place, I noticed several men sitting at an outside counter along one side of the building. I parked and began walking toward the front door, when one of the guys called to me to join them. That's how I became a member of the brotherhood. There were four: Fuss Quarrals, Sam August, N.C. Dupree, and Coop (Cooper) Spence – and now five with me, Al Burke. We meet every morning for breakfast, sitting outside if weather permits.

"Mam, I say Mam. Y'all got our reservation?"

The voice that came through the kitchen window in the back was deep Louisiana.

I yelled back, "Jill, tell that gentleman to have a seat in the bar until something opens up."

N.C. Dupree appeared around the corner of the

building. He was built, as the saying goes, "all in one piece." A quiet confidence inhabited his rugged features that said there was no dispute that couldn't be settled by talking, but if not, that was OK too. N.C. was 78. I'd bet my S.S. check he could still bench press 200 pounds. He was my best friend.

N.C. lived two blocks to the south and always took a shortcut through the yoga studio's parking lot that backed up to the Bayo. Slowly following him at the end of a long, heavy rope was his mournful hound, Itch.

"I see you've gone and bought Itch a new leash," Sam said.

"Hell man, this 'ere's no ordinary leash that you can just go out and buy. This 'ere's the anchor cable off Tony Toutoni's yacht. Can you imagine all the carrying-on this rope has seen?""

"And who is Tony Toutoni?" I asked.

"Famous playboy dude," Jill supplied. "He was called the 'King of Instagram' because of all the pictures he posted of hot party scenes. Is that true about the rope, N.C.?"

"Don't begin to believe a word that man says," I warned.

He gazed sincerely into her innocent blue eyes and said, "Jill, there's two kinds of truth. One's the only kind the unimaginative home builder knows and the other's the kind a poet knows."

Laughing, we all looked down at the disputed leash. Itch thought we were laughing at him and with an even more mournful expression, slumped to the ground.

Coop Spence walked up.

"Don't tell me, let me guess. I just missed round

five-thousand and two of the ongoing duel between Midwest common sense and Cajun mendacity.

Cajun mendacity, I liked that. "Now Coop, you be the judge . . ."

"Never! My doctor ordered me to avoid stress. Where's Fuss?"

"We don't know," Sam answered. "I drove by his house and saw that his car was gone."

Coop was the youngest of our group—seventy. He had retired from the *Chicago Tribune* two years ago where he had written a column on national politics. He'd picked up a Pulitzer for a piece he'd done in his early years about contract kick-back fraud in the city government. Coop was the observer of our group; his arch humor summarizing a discussion. He was nearly bald, had a ready smile and wore rimless half-glasses toward the middle of his nose. He worked out regularly and it showed.

"Are you going to wait for Fuss?" asked Jill, holding an egg in her hand.

We looked at one another. We didn't want to start without him, but . . .

With a decisive move Jill crossed the Rubicon and broke the egg onto the griddle. She knew our orders by heart.

The question about whether we should start without him renewed the question of where Fuss might be.

"Did anyone see him after breakfast yesterday?" Sam asked.

"I did,' volunteered Coop. "At Hansen's. I'd gone to pick up the wine I'd had Becky order for me. He was shopping for groceries. I thought he looked troubled – even more than he has recently, so I asked him – asked what was wrong. It was all about that son-in-law of his, Vince DeSalle. Seems he got fired from the job Fuss got for him at a Suttons Bay realtor. The broker said Vince had alienated the other salespeople. Same old story - screw the other guy – only Vince counts. Fuss was concerned for his daughter Carla's sake, of course, and was trying to think of another job contact for Vince. We parted on that note, but I'm pretty sure he'd said, 'See you tomorrow'."

"I don't know Vince well. What's your impression?" I asked looking from one to the other.

"I wouldn't trust him with the loan of a shovel," answered N.C., "And if he did bring it back, I'd check to see if it still worked."

Coop gave the question more thought. "His dishonesty has a curious quality. As if his being here involves a grand deception. Like he's an undercover spy."

Coop was joking, but I knew what he was getting at.

"Going through the motions of being interested in others," he added.

"It doesn't seem likely that Fuss's problem with Vince can account for his not being here. I mean, it's too early to be out looking for a new job for the guy," I said.

"Equally strange to his not being here is the fact that he hasn't called to explain why," N.C. added.

"It will be a damn shame if he doesn't show up," N.C. went on. "I'm counting on the money you owe me, Sam, from yesterday's bets."

"I owe nothing until Fuss does the math and says I owe you."

"Baloney. I was winner in all three matches."

"It's not over until the fat lady sings and the fat lady is named Fuss Quarrals."

It was the Wimbledon tournament this time, but depending on the season, it could be any sport. Our betting is complicated for the fun of it: including such things as the number of double faults, aces etc. In football season, yards penalized, turnovers and so on. An accountant was required to do the calculating. That was Fuss. He had been one in his former life and now again in retirement. If you had a good day, you could win enough to pay for a haircut.

N.C. took his phone out. "Carla's number is in here. I'll call her. She may know where he is."

"Isn't it a little early?" I objected.

"I'm pretty sure she'd be up." He looked around at our doubtful faces. "OK, I'll wait until we've eaten."

You may think our concern was excessive—that we were making too much of someone being late for breakfast. I can assure you that the group's reaction was entirely reasonable if you knew the locked-in rigidity of Fuss's habits. His not being here or not calling to explain was as unlikely as the IRS forgetting your name.

Jill began putting the plates of food on the counter and my friends and I turned to the business of breakfast. Except for a few exchanges about passing the salt and ketchup, nothing much more was said, until, wiping his mouth with a paper napkin and dropping it on his empty plate, N.C. announced, "I'm calling Carla now."

We all nodded agreement and he dialed.

"Morning Carla, this is N.C. Dupree. How are you? . . . That's great. The reason I called is I need to talk to your dad. Do you know where he is this morning? .

. . No, he's not here. I guess he must have had some errand to run this morning."

N.C. listened to her. She was surprised her dad wasn't with us. She'd spoken to him the previous afternoon and he'd only mentioned he was doing research on what new water heater to buy. Alarm had entered N.C.'s voice as he hurriedly said, "I'm sure it's nothing. I'm sure . . . yeah, of course." He then gave her his phone number.

N.C. hung up and explained. "She's afraid he may have had an accident and she's calling her cousin, Scott, who's a sheriff's deputy here in the county to see if there has been a report of one. Going to call me back." Looking chagrined, he added, "I'm afraid my call did make her worry."

"It made good sense to call her," Coop reassured him.

Jill, who'd stopped to listen to N.C.'s call, now got busy gathering empty dishes, while my friends and I sat and waited for Carla's call. Finally, N.C.'s phone buzzed and all of us focused our attention on him. The news could be read first on his face as it relaxed in relief.

"Yeah, well that's great news. Sure, I'll tell him to call you if I see him before you do and please do the same if you happen to contact him first. Thanks, Carla."

Sam had his phone out and pressed the speed dial for Van's Garage in Leland. "I'm calling J.P. at the Garage. Maybe . . . No, what's wrong with me. They won't be open on the Fourth of July."

I then said the obvious. "We'll just have to wait until he surfaces and explains. I sure hope his briefcase and his calculations deciding who won a fortune this week are in a safe place."

"Once more you've cut to the heart of the matter, Al," said Coop.

As Jill collected what we owed her, I said, "N.C. and I are going to the parade in Leland. Why don't you two join us?"

Sam shook his head. "Natalie's at her sister's in Bloomfield Hills. I'm driving down there right now. They're having a party tonight, but I hope to get in nine holes before that."

"How about you, Coop?"

"I'll be at the parade - because I'm *in* the parade."

"In the parade? What does that mean?"

With a teasing smile, he answered, "You'll just have to wait and see."

I hung back a moment as the others departed. Leaning across the counter I said to Jill's back, "I'm sorry about Pete."

As I turned away from the counter, I noticed that Fuss's coffee was still sitting there – now cold.

# 2

Pedaling up the driveway to my house, I saw Kato, the cat I share my house with. He was waiting for me on the top porch step. He does that whenever I've gone away on my bike—not so when I take the car. Doubts about my cycling skill?

He was standing next to a plastic container. I needn't open it to know what was inside—some variety of delicious cookie left by my neighbor, Susi Springer, probably still warm from an early morning baking session. She was a delight. I wish I'd been home.

A pasture with two milk cows separated our homes. Both she and her husband, Jeff, who worked for the County Road Commission, were a blessing and a problem for me. They eagerly offered to help me anyway they could and Jeff being a strong young guy could be very useful, of course, but giving in to their offers of help also led me to feel older and more depleted than I was. I knew it was easy to adopt such a self-image if encouraged by those around you. I'd seen it happen to my father-in-law. Susi on the other hand, was intent on treating me very lovingly. I couldn't find a problem with that. She took care of their two small kids, two cows, volunteered at a charity resale shop in Lake Leelanau and, of course, ran the household. She was cheerful, bright, compassionate, innovative and possessed uncommonly good common sense. I was saddened and irritated by my conviction that Jeff didn't appreciate how lucky he was. I would say things like, "Susi's one of a kind." He would acknowledge my remark as if I'd commented on the weather. Damn it! How could I make him see how valuable these years are? Had I, you might ask, recognized this truth when Mary and I were the same age as the Springers? Honestly - I had.

I busied myself with my morning routine: make the bed, empty the litter box, water the three cedars I'd planted in the spring and roll the garbage container out to the road. Today was "garbage day", but the pick-up would be delayed until tomorrow, because of the holiday. Yet it had to be done today, you see, since I might forget to do it tomorrow.

Yes, it was a holiday, but neither of my kids and their families would be here. Usually, they all make it here for the Fourth, but this year my son-in-law's family had a reunion in the East. My son, daughter-in-law and grandson had gone camping with friends. It would be the first breakfast cooked out in the open for the eight-year-old. That was all good and I wouldn't want it any other way - still.

At one o'clock, I took the six-pack I'd bought out

of the refrigerator and headed for N.C.'s. He lived with his twin sister, Ruth Ann. Her husband had been the postmaster for the village of Lake Leelanau for many years until his death ten years ago.

The Dupree family went back many generations in New Orleans. After N.C. graduated with a degree in engineering from Tulane, he'd been married for a very short time to a woman he has referred to on rare occasions as "Lil Bit." That experience, he claimed, confirmed his previously held suspicion that he was destined to be a bachelor, so he "never experimented with that institution again." He'd enjoyed a full and comfortable life in Louisiana, retiring as Director of Public Works for Jefferson Parish. A full life until, as Bobby Burns pointed out, our plans may "gang aft a-gley." He became a lonely guy as friends died and others moved away to be closer to children. After her husband died, Ruth Ann began urging him to move in with her in her Lake Leelanau home. He'd visited several times over the years and liked it here. He'd always got on well with his sister, so six years ago he'd made the move. It's been a good decision.

He was wearing a Saints T-shirt and shorts. Notwithstanding shrinkage, he was still six foot. He'd been Tulane's right tackle in the late fifties. I've heard him refer to that team, smiling and shaking his head, as "us po lil lambs." I've respected his obvious wish to leave the subject of the team's record in the past and never researched it, but I'd expect to find those were miserable years for the "Green Wave." To protect his nearly bald head from the sun N.C. wore an old, faded-blue baseball cap that had the word "Bluebell" stitched across the front. I asked him once what Bluebell was about, to which he whipped the cap off, looked at the name and said, "Well I'll be damned," and put the cap back on.

As I said, we were best friends. We'd clicked immediately when we'd first met.

The Fourth of July parade in Leland is a big deal – a big, jolly, funky thing that draws people from miles away. An hour before the three o'clock start, almost every foot of Main Street had already been claimed by various forms of seating, but because of our reserved chairs at our friends' house, we could afford to arrive exactly on time just like V.I.P.s.

After I'd picked up N.C., we'd driven around the north end of Lake Leelanau so we could approach Leland from that direction. We knew there would be a traffic snarl coming from the south. We still had to park a quarter mile from town. From the hill at the north end of Main Street we could view its entire length—an ant nest of people on the move in all directions. Along the curb ran an uninterrupted line of folding lawn chairs, camp stools and spread-out blankets. N.C. and I worked our way through the happy throng shaking hands and slapping the backs of those we knew. That was a small percentage, since the majority were tourists. Two blocks along the way we came to "The Merc" – The Leland Mercantile Co., a vintage establishment that might have sold Fourth of July hotdogs to your great grandmother. We stopped here and looked directly across the street at the judges' stand, a temporary platform from which the three honorary judges would select the "Best in Parade" float. They were already seated and working on assuming their impartial judicial attitudes. One judge was our friend Dolly Hansen, but we were both chiefly interested in getting a good look at this year's celebrity, Bethany Parker, the past U.N. Ambassador. She was in town visiting her good friend and former college classmate, Carole Stuart, a fact supplied us by our local paper, *Leelanau Enterprise.*

"Nice looking lady," said N.C. "Nice to see her smiling. As I remember her in pictures when she was Ambassador, she always looked like she'd eaten a bad lunch. She's certainly aged better than we have."

"Yeah, but she's at least five years younger than we are."

"You're not going to claim we looked that good five years ago."

Looking back to the judges' stand, he continued, "Back when the 'MeToo' movement was going strong – when every woman with any status who'd experienced sexual assault wanted to tell her own story to help bring its frequency to public awareness, I remember she also made a MeToo claim."

"What had happened to her?"

"I don't remember. I don't think it was anything current at that time - like from earlier in her life."

I searched my memory. Nothing.

We continued through the crowd until we got to our friends Tim's and Betty's house. Half-a-dozen people we knew well greeted us and Jim removed picnic supplies from the two chairs he was saving for us. The mood as usual for this event was one of childlike hilarity, as if we were all about to mount and ride donkeys or don silly party hats.

A blast from the fire engine's horn and siren flattened all conversation. Make no mistake, the parade had begun! We stood at attention for the honor guard of aging veterans and remained standing for four beautiful palominos ridden by officers of the Chippewa/Ottawa tribal police, each grasping the staff of an American flag. Corny? Yeah, but it still caused a chill to run down my spine. In years past, the next marcher would have been Leland's own, authentic, white-bearded Uncle Sam, walking proud. Alas, being authentic, the parade route had become just too damn long for him. He was missed. Next, of course, came the decorated bikes— maybe one hundred. Some were the product of imagination and effort, but most were last-minute jobs. From our viewing position a third of the way along the route, I judged only a quarter of the tricycles would make it to the half-way mark. What enthusiasm there had been at the beginning had waned and now only parental urging kept the wheels turning. The seriously lagging had to be lifted - tricycle and all - to the sidelines, because . . . Here comes the band!

They were a happy crew of musicians from all walks, from visiting first-chair symphony players to high school band members past and present. I even spotted three members of a Detroit jazz group that happened to be playing a gig in Traverse City. They all wore T-shirts printed with the full display of gold braid. There were two numbers in their repertoire: "Strike Up the Band" and "It's a Grand Old Flag." The majorette was a very pretty barista from a local coffee house. Her costume just met the minimal requirement – her prance was uninhibited. A cup of coffee from her hands would never be the same again.

The serious competition was among the several floats that had decided to make an extra effort to win first prize this year. The Leland Township Public Library was the first in line. A librarian was reading to a group of spellbound young kids sitting on cushions on the floor looking up at her—Story Hour.

"The judges will have a hard time not voting for that one," N.C. observed.

I was still smiling at the library float when the Chamber of Commerce entry demanded full attention. A speedboat pulled a bikini-clad water skier chased by a giant salmon, its sharp-toothed mouth snapping at her rear. A sign read, "Enjoy the Salt-free, Shark-free Great Lakes."

Coming along next was the familiar wrecker from Van's Garage, the business that kept the county's wheels turning. I bent over to grab a beer and when I looked up again, I saw that the wrecker was pulling a decrepit convertible missing its hood. Sitting atop the engine, mallet and chisel in hand was a clown. Another clown leaned in holding a huge book, the word, "Manual" on its cover. The first clown consulted the manual a moment and then applied mallet and chisel to the engine, whereupon he'd consult the book again then, seriously return to his work.

"It's Coop!" screamed N.C. "Like he said, he's in the parade!"

And so it was. There sat our friend, mammoth red nose, wild orange hair and turned down corners of a determined mouth concentrating on his desperately serious work.

Complaining about his efforts, two "women" clowns occupied the car's front seat. The passenger swung a large purse at the two mechanics, while the driver held up the steering wheel, appealing to the crowd along the street for help. Styrofoam nuts and bolts fell continuously out the rear onto the pavement where two frustrated clowns - frequently getting in each other's way - swept them up.

"They've got to take first prize," I shouted above everyone's laughter.

After the clowns, I couldn't give the rest of the floats a fair appraisal. The parade ended, but our friends' party went on until supper time. It was then, that N.C. and I looked at each other at the same moment with the same thought – we hadn't heard anything about Fuss.

"I'd like to call Carla," N.C. said. "But, if she hasn't heard from him, my call might add to her worry."

"I think you're right, and she did say she'd call you."

"Yeah, and she would too. So, what shall we do?"

"Let's drive by his place." It was something to do.

We walked back to where I'd parked my car. Now, it was sitting all alone, the other cars having left hours ago. We drove back around Lake Leelanau to Fuss's place. His single story four-bedroom house had two hundred feet of frontage on the lake. He'd built it thirty years ago when his family of four was intact. At that time, it had been a vacation home far away from Florida's summer heat. That's when he was VP in charge of the actuarial division of a national life insurance company. His personality must have fit that job like skin fits the body. His house and other possessions reflected this: nothing in excess, the best reasonable selection of essentials and everything in its place. Now, just Fuss and his dog, Oscar, lived here.

"Well, his Jeep isn't here," said N.C. as I pulled into the driveway.

"Maybe it's in the garage."

"He never puts his car in the garage until the weather starts to get nasty. But, yeah, maybe."

"I'll take a peek through the side window," N.C. said, opening the car door.

He was shaking his head as he walked back.

"That takes care of that. He's out and about," I said as he settled back into the seat next to me.

"Shouldn't we be sure he isn't inside – had a stroke or something."

"I see what you mean; and somebody came and stole his car while he was helpless," I said in mock agreement.

Before I could start the car, my phone rang. It was Sam, calling from Bloomfield Hills.

"I just got down here. Have you heard anything from Fuss yet?"

"No. N.C. and I are at his house right now. I checked his garage – no car."

"Fucking square one!"

"Right. We're just going to have to wait 'til tonight. He's sure to be at Kirby Spence's party. I heard him accept her invitation."

"I remember his saying that too," Sam said, "and Fuss would never – make that could never renege on an invitation he'd accepted. Natalie and I are driving back tonight. I'll see you in the morning."

The lady we were talking about, Kirby Spence, was Coop's aunt. She was one of the county's grand dames. She had grown up in Leland. After graduating from high school here she had gone on to Northwestern where she met a guy named Raymond Spence. This was followed up with forty-five years of happily splitting their married years between Chicago, where Ray was an architect, and Leland, where they built a house on a bluff overlooking Lake Michigan. Ray has not been with her for more than twenty years since his heart attack at a Bull's game during the 1998 NBA finals. After he died, Kirby sold the house in Chicago and moved back to her hometown, giving her energy to the institutions serving the county's needs. She was ninety now, and while fully in command of her cerebral assets, she had to ration her energy, limiting herself to The Little Garden Club, the League of Women Voters and the Knitting Cabal.

Since moving back to Leland, she had given a Fourth of July party every year, inviting everyone she knew. The guest list had grown over the years. It was an easy party to put on she claimed, just booze, catered hotdogs and baked beans and a view of the fireworks over Leland's harbor. The same menu for years until she'd had to add a choice of gluten-free hotdog buns.

I picked up N.C. and Ruth Ann and drove to the party. Kirby had enlisted some young guys to park cars thus avoiding chaos. The house was large, but not palatial. The back deck, however, was large enough to accommodate the entire cast and chorus of Verdi's Aïda - chariots and horses included. And there was space in the yard beyond the deck for half the Met's audience. Here in the county, guests arrived at the time stated on an invitation. Back In Detroit, 8 o'clock meant 8:15 at the earliest.

Coop and his wife, Joan, were acting as assistant hosts. Before I could put together a smart remark about his clown act in the parade, he beat me.

"No! Please don't start describing the strange noises you're hearing in your old Civic. We're here to party."

"But it will only take a minute. It's right outside. Go get your mallet."

He turned from me and kissed Ruth Ann on the cheek and I got a kiss from Kirby.

"Has Fuss come yet," I asked.

"Not yet," Coop replied, a note of dread in his voice.

We moved on into the party and began mixing. And what a mix was here tonight. Brief words with guys from my book group. We'd met only a few nights ago, where there was as much discussion about our country going to hell as about the book we'd read. The active businesspeople of the community were here as well as the orchardists representing all flavors of fruit except citrus. And then there were all the retirees, living quietly modest lives now, but real earth movers not long ago. Everyone was on a first name footing and everyone was treated equally. It was the best of all possible worlds - this evening.

It was getting dark enough for the Leland fireworks to begin and people were moving out onto the deck and lawn. I cast a glance around to see if I could spot Fuss. No luck. I went out and found a place at the deck railing, holding a very full glass of very good Scotch. How had that happened? On my right, I became aware of and exchanged greetings with a tennis friend, "Down the line Hugh." We kidded each other for a moment and then I turned to my left and looked into the eyes of a very attractive woman. She smiled and I was shocked into near sobriety. She was our former Ambassador, Beth Parker.

What to say? "Hi", seemed weak. Can I get you

something to drink came to mind and that's what came out of my mouth.

"No, thank you."

I then evolved into a whiskey-loosened mood. "Then would you please help me with mine?" I raised the near-full glass of Scotch. "I have way too much here, and I find it very difficult to throw away Scotch this good."

"I understand completely," she said and reached for the glass and took a healthy swallow.

"Thanks for your help."

"Thank you. This is good Scotch."

I understood why she was chosen to be an ambassador – immediate, sympathetic and diplomatic response resting on good judgment.

"I'm Al Burke."

"Beth Parker"

"It's a pleasure to meet you—I mean a real pleasure, since I appreciate the work you've done for us."

She nodded slightly and slightly smiled, took another sip of the Scotch and handed me the glass.

"Aside from the serious undertaking of being a parade judge, I heard you are also visiting an old college friend, who is also a friend of mine."

"Yes, my roommate at college, Carole Stuart."

"Is this the first time you've been here?"

"Yes, and from what I've seen so far, I believe what she's been telling me for years; you have a real slice of heaven here – and I'll only tell people everyone will like."

We both laughed. What can I say, I liked this lady and in my loosened mood, I was on the point of telling her so, when the first star shell burst over Leland Harbor and the show was on, accompanied by the "Oh's" and "Ah's" from Kirby's party.

With the dependably furious finale filling the sky, the guests erupted into cheers and then began the movement toward departure attended by the familiar and pleasant reminders that they would meet again: tomorrow at Trish's, or Thursday on the golf course, or sooner, or sometime.

For Beth Parker and me it was, "Enjoyed talking to you." Any rational basis for a future contact was absent and we both left it there – sadly on my part. I wanted to believe she shared the same feeling.

In the living room, I saw N.C. and Ruth searching faces for mine and I waved and walked their way.

"Looked serious to me," N.C. said.

Puzzled I asked, "What?"

"You and the guest of honor."

"Ha," I laughed.

Soberly, he said, "Fuss never came. I just checked with Coop."

"Not good. We can't kid ourselves any longer about a harmless answer."

All the clowns and marching bands and fireworks couldn't alter the dread we shared.

# 3

My eyes adjusted to the rectangle of gray light. There were drops of water on the glass, running one after the other down to the bottom of the window. Other drops then loaded up with moisture and followed. It was a rainy day. I watched this process for a while judging the rain's tempo. A slow, lazy rain. An all-day rain. I sat up and yawned. No bike ride to Caballo Bayo today. We'll be eating inside. No hurry. It was only four minutes by car. I walked to the window and looked out into the misty drizzle. Mother Nature was taking a day off from supplying tourists with sunshine.

I shuffled into the bathroom and looked in the mirror at a face that'd had too much Scotch the night before – a graphic reprimand. "Point taken," I conceded to the face. After dressing, I began the search for my car keys. Once found, I skipped asking myself to account for them being on top of the refrigerator. The phone rang as I was about to leave.

"Al, I'm glad I caught you at home," said a somber N.C. "Stay there. I'm picking you up. I'm at the Bayo and I just heard from Fuss's nephew, the cop, Buddy. Carla asked him to make contact with us . . . they found Fuss . . . he was in his boat—dead."

This was too much, way too much to process. It was as if I'd been listening to soft jazz which had suddenly changed to cymbals of a marching band.

"What?"

"In his boat at the Nothport marina. They think he fell down the companionway ladder. I'm coming to pick you up. Sam just arrived and he's going to wait for Coop and then drive up."

A sudden punch in the gut. Later, I was able to analyze the meaning his death had for me, but right then only profound loneliness enveloped me. In time, I'd let myself see how our breakfast club had become a quasi-family, a group I trusted and belonged to. Fuss's death scuttled complacent sureness just as my wife, Mary's, death had. There was no certainty; every moment was up for grabs. It was that dark emptiness I felt as I hung up the phone. N.C.'s arrival was very welcome.

Fuss Quarrals's one extravagance was his sailboat. He'd had it for a long time, purchased when his daughter was a teen, and his sister and her family also still lived in the area. Family fun. Thirty-eight feet I think he'd said. I forget the make. I'm not very interested in boats. Fuss had taken us guys out a couple of times for cruises on the big lake, but it was clear he'd lost interest in the boat, particularly since one of Carla's daughters had a true phobia for it. He'd never mentioned using it recently and certainly never on his own.

"I wonder what he was doing on the boat?" I said as I closed the car door.

N.C. just shook his head in a way that meant total puzzlement.

"Did they say when they thought this happened – when he fell?"

"No. I told you all I know."

N.C. took Eagle Highway north to M22 and then on north toward Northport.

"I don't think I've heard him say anything about that boat since we all went out on it the last time . . . summer before last. I'd forgotten he had it," I ruminated aloud.

"You're right. I think he'd sell it only it still signifies good times he'd had when the whole family was together."

Northport was another one of the peninsula's perfect villages – maybe the most perfect. The central street and its one and two-story frame buildings rolled downhill like a broad welcoming-carpet to a large, well-laid-out marina. I registered nothing of this quaint beauty this morning. I focused only on the sheriff's cars parked at odd angles around the marina's entrance. Traffic cones had been set up to close it to cars, so N.C. parked on the main street. The rain had paused when we got out of the car. We walked over to a sheriff's deputy standing guard at the marina entrance.

'Hi officer, I'm N.C. Dupree. My friend, Al Burke, and I are good friends of Frank Quarrals, the man who had the accident. We'd like to learn more about what happened."

She was short and trim, making the large gun, holster, radio and what all she carried look like a burden, but she seemed unfazed.

"I just arrived here," she said. "I was told it looks like your friend was going fishing and tripped going down the companionway ladder and hit his head."

"Fishing?" I blurted. "What makes them think that?"

She shrugged. "You'd better wait until the undersheriff is finished out there and ask him," she said motioning toward the docks.

"How about us going out there to talk to him?" N.C. suggested.

"Not now. No one is allowed beyond this point right now."

I remembered which was Fuss's boat—fourth slip out on the second dock, the "B" dock. I could see several men standing on the deck. One was gesturing freely as he talked.

"Is that the undersheriff waving his arms about?" I asked the young woman, pointing at the dock.

The deputy, the name on a pin above her badge read, Deputy Sarah Carlson, turned to look where I pointed. "Yes, that's him, Jeff Payne." There was a smile playing around the corners of her mouth as she added, "Spelled, P-A-Y-N-E."

Coop and Sam arrived now.

"No trespassing beyond this young deputy," N.C. explained.

I spoke to her. "We'd like to get word to Sheriff Payne that we want to speak to him."

"Sure," she said, taking the radio transceiver off her belt.

I couldn't hear what she said, but I presumed she was telling one of the other cops to give Payne the message. I saw one of them look briefly in our direction.

Just then, a man's back appeared at the head of the companionway steps. He climbed backward onto the deck hauling something heavy after him. I saw, then, the black body bag, followed by another guy. For a minute they worked at deck level, then they stood up holding the shafts of a collapsible stretcher. They made their way off the boat, extended the wheels from the stretcher and set it down on the dock. They, then, rolled it off the dock and lifted it into the rear of the ambulance that was parked nearby on the grass at the end of the pier.

I noticed that the undersheriff continued his conversation with the others all through this procedure. We watched the ambulance drive slowly away with our friend.

My attention returned to observing Payne more closely. His body language and gestures resembled someone swapping stories at a bar rather than a serious discussion about a tragic death. He and the others began laughing hard. What could be so damn funny?

I began moving forward while I said, "I'm sorry Deputy Carlson, but the sheriff's not engaged in police business. Call him and tell him we're coming to talk to him."

She raised her hand to stop me, but I pushed past with the other guys tight behind me. She gave up and again turned to her radio.

Payne got the message we were coming, and he wasn't happy. I noticed him directing another deputy to head us off. This man walked toward us, prepared for some mild crowd control – Please folks, stay back on the curb. Alarm replaced his confident expression as he understood that we wouldn't be listening.

As we met him Coop announced, "We want to speak to the person who's in charge here."

Payne did assess the situation correctly then and decided not to engage in warfare he was sure to lose in front of his assembled audience. He climbed off the boat and onto the dock.

"How can I help you? I'm Undersheriff Payne . . . and you are?"

Coop did the introductions.

"Frank Quarrals was a very good friend of ours. We'd like an account of what happened to him."

The man's manner loudly expressed the notion that he was a phenomenon to be appreciated. He was drunk with the fact that he was "The Man" at this event. He gave Coop the smile of the adult who was going to kindly explain to a child that water ran downhill – in simple terms that would leave out complicated concepts like gravity.

"Ordinarily we don't speak to the public about the details of a death until it has been thoroughly investigated, but in this case the facts are very clear.

"Mr. Quarrals was going fishing. He came here before dawn planning to get an early start. It was dark and he tripped going down the ladder and fell and hit his head on the corner of the table down inside the cabin. Probably got a skull fracture."

"This morning?" N.C. asked puzzled.

"No. Yesterday morning. The Medical Examiner," He made a head-motion toward one of the men standing on the deck – "thinks he's been dead at least twenty-four hours."

"Why do you think he was going fishing?" asked N.C., still puzzled.

Payne was becoming impatient. He had not intended to be open to questions from us. He had descended from the deck to demonstrate to the men on the boat his "touch with the people" by briefly and smoothly placating the oldsters and sending them on their way.

"For one thing," he explained grudgingly as he turned to climb back on the deck, "he brought his fishing rods and tackle box."

"But Fuss never went fishing alone and he was expected at breakfast with us yesterday morning. He would have told us if he wasn't coming. It doesn't make sense."

I think he was just going to ignore my remarks, but N.C. said, "How 'bout that mister?"

That steady unwavering challenge I'd seen in N.C.'s eyes on a few other occasions was there. You understood what it must have been like to face him across a scrimmage line. Payne, while thirty years younger, blinked.

"It would have been a helluva lot better for him if he hadn't stood you guys up, but the facts speak for themselves. He packed himself a lunch, got his fishing gear together and came to his boat. He was climbing down into the cabin with his lunch in his hand when he tripped and fell. He hit his head on the corner of the table and it killed him." He emphatically turned now and reboarded Fuss's boat.

"Officer," I called up to him, "Have you notified his daughter? Carla DeSalle?"

He turned part way to face me. "Of course."

I wasn't satisfied and I knew the others weren't either. I didn't know what else to say right then and clearly this self-important jerk was happy with his conclusion and wasn't about to listen to any objection from us. We began to slowly leave the dock and walk back to our cars.

"I wonder who found him," said Coop.

"Yeah, I wonder," I repeated. "Probably not the police. They'd have no reason to be looking into boats here in the marina. Maybe one of the other boat owners."

"Or someone who works here," added N.C.

Our heads turned in unison toward the kiosk on the end of the first dock, Dock "A", where the harbormaster had an office. The silhouette of a person could be seen moving inside.

Coop said, "I've met him. Name's Jim. He's a friend of Kirby's"

We walked the length of the dock and Coop opened the door. You could see that the guy recognized Coop but couldn't place him.

"Hi, I'm Coop Spence, Kirby Spence's nephew. We met on a Conservancy hike. You're Jim, right?"

"That's right. How's it going?"

"Well, not too well at the moment, Jim. Frank Quarrals was a good friend of ours." He looked out the office window toward Fuss's boat as he said this.

"That so. I'm sorry. I've known Fuss for many years, although I haven't seen too much of him lately. Seems only his daughter and her husband use the boat now, and then only occasionally. I think I remember you fellows going out with Fuss. Was it last year?"

"Actually, summer before last."

"Do you happen to know how his body was discovered?" I asked, anxious to push ahead.

"Yes, I found him – sad to say."

A glance at our faces told him we wanted the whole detailed story.

"I recognized his car, the Jeep, and the bumper sticker, 'All Americans Are Immigrants – Except Those From Peshawbestown.' It was parked there – the lot at the south end of the marina when I came to work yesterday morning – on the Fourth. But I paid no further attention to it then. The marina was busy. Right here on this dock a rowdy party on one of the boats demanded my attention. This morning when I saw that the Jeep was in the same spot it made me wonder. I looked over to Dock 'B' where I knew his boat was moored and saw that the cabin hatch was open, so I thought I'd walk over there and say hello. I called to him from the walkway alongside the slip but got no answer. So, I climbed aboard, still expecting to find him working down in the cabin. Instead, I was shocked to see him crumpled at the bottom of the ladder. I went down and realized immediately he was dead."

He looked from one to the other of us with, I'm sure, what must be a universal apology for not having been able to do more, as if no death would happen if someone had done the right thing at the right time.

Sam felt the need to reassure him. "Accidents happen. What could you have done?"

"The police believe he was intending to go fishing," I said. "Was there anything that you saw that would go along with that?"

Jim concentrated, calling to mind the visual impression he'd had upon first boarding the boat.

"There were two fishing rods lying on the deck and a tackle box. I guess he'd been carrying his lunch in a small cooler. It had come open when he fell and a sandwich in a baggie was there on the floor of the cabin." He silently thought for another quarter minute and then concluded, "That's about it."

I had to admit that this supported the lone-outing scenario.

Sam asked, "You noticed his car parked here yesterday morning. How about the night before, the night of the third?"

"I wasn't here when the office closed at eight. I left at five in the afternoon. I didn't notice his Jeep, but I wouldn't really have paid attention to the cars that were here."

"Is there a night watchman here at the marina?" asked Sam.

"No, there isn't."

Coop looked to the rest to see if anyone else had a question and then thanked Jim for his help. We walked back to our cars.

Sam suggested, "I don't know about you guys, but I could use some breakfast."

"Me too," I agreed. "The Tribune is just a block from here."

Four friends sat searching the faces of one another for some beginning to a way out of the awful feelings of grief. To lose a close friend in any way can be an overwhelming blow. To lose him to violence of any sort adds the element of fear. While huge, it's still something one can slowly get one's arms around. Reality must be accepted. If, however, there is an element that renders that reality ambiguous, like "missing in action," confusion is added which threatens to defeat one's capacity to deal with grief. What we knew of Fuss's habits – solid facts to us – made the story we'd just heard at the marina unreal.

Sam contributed, "Maybe there was someone who was going to go out with him."

Now there was an idea we hadn't considered. Probably because we would have expected him to tell us about it beforehand. Yes, that would address our certainty that he wouldn't have taken the boat out alone.

"No!" I said, shaking my head emphatically. "That won't work. If there had been this other person, he would have either been there when Fuss fell and would have gone or called for help, or he would have come along later and discovered Fuss and done the same thing. That didn't happen."

"Right," said N.C. "That puts us back to square one."

"You mean back to where we've proven Fuss didn't do what he did do," Sam said sarcastically.

"Correction," I protested. "Didn't do what Payne said he did."

"People don't always do what you expect," Sam countered.

"You're right, people don't – but Fuss always did," said Coop laughing.

"What about the sheriff? I mean the real sheriff – Sheriff Davis. That's his name, right? He has a good reputation. Anyone know him?" I asked."

"I've talked to him a couple of times," N.C. said. "His nickname is 'Hoss'. He's a giant of a man. That's how he got the name from an old TV western. He's an easy guy to talk to."

That sounded promising to me, We ate our breakfasts, but we continued talking and puzzling over Fuss's alleged actions. We parted back where we'd parked the cars; Sam, driving his Audi, took Coop in the direction of Leland.

N.C. and I got into his Honda. He reached forward to insert the ignition key and then paused. "I feel like we should see Carla – tell her we're sorry for her loss and see if there's something we can do."

"I know what you mean. She lives close to here. Let's go there now."

He started the car and began driving south along the street next to the marina. Suddenly he turned abruptly into the parking lot at the marina's south end.

"There's Fuss's Jeep. Let's take a look."

He pulled up behind the familiar car and we got out. I reread the bumper sticker Fuss had made that proclaimed that we were all immigrants except the residents of Peshawbestown, the Ottawa/Chippewa reservation just south of Northport. I glanced in the rear window at the luggage space. The case containing emergency items was there – as always – but except for that, the space was empty. N.C. tried the front door. It was locked.

"That's odd," he mumbled. "Never seen him do that."

"Carla needs to be told the Jeep's here," I remarked as we got back into his car.

# 4

Carla lived on South Shore Dr. only blocks from the marina. N.C. rang the bell and we both stood dreading our mission.

Vince answered the door. His first reaction – his true reaction – lasted three milliseconds. It said, "These old farts!." It was followed by two seconds of phony welcome which resolved into a suspicious, "Yes?"

"We need to talk to Carla," I answered. "We've just come from the marina. The sheriff said he'd called to tell you the bad news."

"Yeah. He just called." He was deciding how he'd deal with us, when Carla came up behind him. She was wearing a bathrobe. Her face was tear streaked. She had been crying hard.

She stepped past Vince and hugged both N.C. and me. And drew us into the house. I don't remember all the exact words that followed, but I could see as we were leaving, she had accepted the idea of Fuss going fishing that she'd heard from Undersheriff Payne. We didn't argue with her.

"What about Oscar?" she asked suddenly.

Surprised, N.C. answered, "I don't know."

"You're sure he wasn't at the boat?" she said anxiously. "Even if Dad only went to the boat to do some work, he'd take Oscar along."

"He's probably at the house. We'll go and see and if he's there we'll bring him back here," I offered.

"Please do that," Carla said. "Just a minute and I'll get my key. My father never locked his house, but I'd feel better knowing it's locked now."

Vince walked with us back to the front door, where I thought to tell him that Fuss's Jeep was parked at the marina. Somehow, I got the impression he already knew.

We continued south on M22 past the casino at Peshawbestown and turned to the right in Suttons Bay onto M204. As we passed the Government Center where the Sheriff's Department was located, I said, "We need to talk to Sheriff Davis. After we check on Oscar."

Five minutes later we reached Fuss's house. This was not the same house I had viewed just yesterday. Then it had been my friend's home where I'd spent many enjoyable times. Now it was an alien place, just as the body in the funeral home is not the friend you'd lost. We walked to the front door. It was locked. "Huh," I uttered in surprise. I then took the key Carla had given me and opened the door.

Immediately, we heard the whine coming from

the direction of the kitchen. We hurried there to find that the imperative lament meaning, "I'm in here guys!," came from the other side of the utility room door. N.C. opened the door and Oscar immediately came to him, looking up gratefully while his tail gave irregular wags.

Looking into the utility room, I saw that the water and food bowls were empty. I also saw a puddle of urine and a pile of feces in one corner.

I patted Oscar's head. "That's OK old boy; neither of us could have held it either."

N.C. took Oscar outside. I opened cupboards looking for food then filled the water bowl.

N.C. came back with a happier looking dog. We stood and watched him eagerly lap up the water. N.C. dialed Carla's number and when Vince answered, assured him Oscar was OK and we'd be bringing him to their house soon.

"I don't get it," I said. "Why would Fuss leave Oscar at home if he was going fishing by himself? He knows Oscar enjoys all outings and he's comfortable on the boat. And why confine him here?"

N.C. didn't attempt a reply.

We left Oscar to catch up on lost meals and went back through the kitchen to the main part of the house. The first thing I noticed, looking into the dining room was a cereal bowl and coffee cup on the table. I walked into the room for a better look.

"N.C., look here. He had breakfast at home before he set out for his boat."

"Looks like he wanted to get out on the water sooner than if he'd stopped to have breakfast with us first."

We stared into the soiled bowl as if the surviving

flakes were successful rivals for our friend's loyality.

"Some kinda flakes," N.C. mumbled.

"I never saw him eat cereal at the Bayo," I thought out loud.

My gaze shifted to one of the chairs where a familiar object rested on the seat.

"His briefcase!" I said, taking hold of the handle and lifting it onto the table, then undoing the clasp.

"Should we be opening it? Man's private briefcase," said N.C.

"I need to check something."

I took out the ledger in which Fuss recorded the details of our morning bets: odds, point spreads and so on. I turned to the page dated July 3$^{rd}$. He had done his homework; the results had been calculated for the distribution to be made July 4$^{th}$ – at the breakfast he'd missed. I next removed the liver-colored envelope with the cloth tape tie, the envelope where he kept our cash and opened it. Inside, were five business envelopes, each with the name of one of us written on the outside. In each of these was the slip of paper on which Fuss described the outcome of that person's bets. Two of the envelopes contained cash—the winners. In two, Fuss had placed a note that read, "Better luck next time." - his usual condolence. All had been in readiness for breakfast on July 4$^{th}$.

"Fuss wouldn't have had all this ready, if he hadn't planned to come to breakfast with us as usual," I pronounced with finality.

"He could have done it just to get it out of the way before he went off fishing," came the half-hearted reply.

Oscar joined us as we wandered down a hall into

Fuss's bedroom. The bed had not been slept in. Oscar's bed was against the wall. He went there and gave a stuffed animal a nudge with his nose.

A red-light blinked on an answering machine on the small desk that stood against the wall. It indicated five messages.

I punched the "playback" button saying, "One shouldn't listen to other people's machines – except this time."

The first message was from Vince at 6:40 p.m. on July 3rd. "I need to talk to you sometime tomorrow. I'm sorry for what happened at the agency. It wasn't my fault. The other salesmen are clods and afraid of anyone with energy. Anyway, I'm in Grand Rapids tonight at the Sunrise Motor Lodge. I plan to get a sales agreement in the morning on a sale I made. I don't want that commission stolen. I'll call tomorrow." The second message was Sam, recorded at 8:10 p.m. on the 3rd. "Fuss, I need to talk to you again. Call me." The third message was N.C. at 7:34 a.m. on the 4th. "Wondering where you are. Call me." That was the call he made from Caballo Bayo. The fourth and fifth were Carla's calls asking her father to call her. That was after N.C. had called her from Caballo Bayo yesterday morning.

We moved to the bathroom where I turned on the light. All was spic and span – almost polished. I opened the shower door and looked inside. An almost new bar of soap in the dish, back brush hanging from a hook on the wall, bottle of shampoo on the floor. A faint smell of Comet pervaded. I turned off the light and turned to leave almost tripping over Oscar.

On the way back down the hall, I paused to look into Fuss's study – again a picture of order. We went on back to the living room, prepared to leave.

"There's something we should do," said N.C.

"I know," I agreed. "I'd like to leave it for Vince, but I know he'd have Carla do it."

We returned to the utility room and mopped up the puddle.

N. C. dropped me off at my place and then continued to Carla's with Oscar, dog food and Fuss's house key.

# 5

Kato was standing at the front steps. There had been enough that had been abnormal about the morning to make him worry. I greeted him saying I was sorry I'd had to rush off earlier. He didn't give a damn for explanations but was clearly relieved that I'd returned, and life could be expected to resume its routine. He led the way to the front door and waited for me to open it, entering first. He went straight to his food bowl and finished his breakfast.

The original house had been a two-bedroom farmhouse built ninety years ago. It had changed hands several times over those years and each time improvements had been made. A third bedroom and an up-to-date kitchen and bath had been added before my wife and I bought the place. The house sat at the center of the remaining twenty acres of what once had been eighty.

I walked about aimlessly. I figeted. I couldn't bring myself to focus on any activity. Then I remembered Sheriff Davis. "Hoss" Davis, N.C. had called him. The Sheriff's Office was only ten minutes away. I got my car keys, told Kato not to worry, that I'd be back soon and went out to the car and drove to Sheriff's Headquarters.

Behind what was probably a bulletproof glass partition the receptionist was lost in thought. Suddenly startled out of her reverie she looked up at me.

"I'd guess it was a pleasant memory you were reliving," I said. "Fourth of July party?"

She laughed aloud as one does when someone guesses exactly what you'd been thinking.

"Remembering my daughter riding her bike in the parade. What can I do for you?"

"I'd like to talk to Sheriff Davis, if he has time."

"I'm sorry but Sheriff Davis and his wife are on their twentieth anniversary trip to Europe."

"Really?"

"Yes, they left a week ago."

"How long will they be gone?"

She glanced at a calendar on her desk. "Mmm. A little over a week."

"Isn't this a busy time to be away?" I wanted him to be here, so irritation must have been in my voice.

The receptionist heard it and said, "You're right. They had originally scheduled the trip for May, but his mother had to have surgery and they were forced to cancel. But then a group of the County Commissioners pushed Hoss, that's Sheriff Davis, to go ahead and not delay."

I was digesting this as she added, "Undersheriff Payne just came in. Do you want me to see if he's busy?"

"No, no. That's OK," I replied, quickly.

I left the building and stood outside feeling restless. Caballo Bayo was two miles down the road. Another coffee? More caffeine wouldn't quell the restlessness, but I could talk to Jill. She needed to know what we'd encountered at the marina.

Although the rain had stopped, the outside counter and stools were still wet, so I went inside and sat at a table that was off to one side, so I could talk to Jill with some privacy. When she got a chance, she came. Her eyes were still red from crying earlier when she'd first heard about Fuss. She and Fuss had had a special connection. He had been more of a father to her than we others were. She'd suffered two losses in two days. I described the scene at Northport.

"The cops are sure Fuss was going fishing alone and fell and hit his head. The guy in charge, Payne, isn't interested in our objections. He's sure we're just old codgers who can't face facts. It's so damn frustrating! I wish I could think more like Sam. Like, 'Why get all worked up? Fuss is dead and we can't bring him back. That's all that matters.'"

I think my lamenting helped me some. Probably didn't help Jill. I paid her and went home.

I was still uncomfortably restless when I got home. Being outside seemed a better idea than going indoors. I took a couple of deep breaths. Yes, Janette, the exercise leader was right. I took a couple more. I decided, then, to walk the property. I have a well-worn circle route, which I hike frequently enough so that the vegetation has been worn down to the earth and a permanent path established. It's only when the snow gets to be half a foot deep that I give up the circuit until the following spring. From the house extending southward stretches an expanse of grassland. Originally this must have been a cultivated field won from the forest by hard labor. Cutting down trees, pulling up roots. Just to think of such all-out toil made me tired. The path crosses this field while rising on a glacial moraine to the southern border of my land. Here a ridge affords a view into my neighbor's pasture where their two cows stood together. Heading east along the ridge, the path continues into a hardwood forest. At this point, with its back to the trees, a shooting blind had been built, which gave a hunter a downhill view and a clear shot back over the fields. There had been evidence it was still being used when we bought the place. I dismantled it and used some of the material to build a tool shed for Mary's flower garden. I also posted "No Hunting" signs around the property. I'd heard no feedback about either of these moves.

The path continues through the woods, rising and falling with the ancient sand dunes lying beneath the forest floor. This part of my route is the source of about a hundred morel mushrooms each spring. The northeast corner of the property is marked by what must be a virgin white pine at least twelve feet around. It had to have been a natural reference point for those original settlers, saying, "Your land lies to the east of the big tree – mine to the west." My view to the east from here is over another neighbor's cherry orchard. Sometimes I put a sandwich and a beer in my knapsack and come and sit with my back to the tree and eat my lunch—the ghosts of those earlier neighbors sitting with me. Heading back toward the house, the path crosses a sandy stretch covered with sumac before circling my pond. Spring-fed, the pond has no fish, only an abundance of frogs and two mallards that return each spring as if they had a long-term lease. I keep hoping they'll have a family, but no luck so far. What would Kato think of ducklings?

Equanimity reestablished; I was able to put in a useful afternoon working around the house. I made French toast for dinner, my "go to" when I'm very lazy. Then, I picked up my phone to call N.C. to tell him that the real sheriff, Sheriff Davis, was canoodling with his wife somewhere in Europe and wouldn't be back for a week, when the thing buzzed in my hand and the ID said N.C. Dupree.

"I was just about to dial your number," I said answering.

"There's an old saying, 'Great minds think alike.' I was thinking that I had to mow my lawn, which means you were thinking of coming to help me."

"Another 'old saying' bites the dust. Actually, I was calling to say Sheriff Davis isn't around to hear our objection to that ass Payne's conclusion. Davis ran off with his wife to Europe. Do you know anyone else – sheriff's bunch – state police?"

"I'm happy to say I've had no business with the police since I moved here. Back in Louisiana there was a time when I got to know the traffic cops better than I wanted to."

"Same here. I don't know any of the local police. Like you, a regular event in my twenties was looking up into unsmiling eyes and saying, 'I had no idea I was going that fast officer.' Another regular event was running out of gas. Why were we always running out of gas?"

"Assuming you were like me, you could only afford to buy a buck's worth at a time. That makes for a lot of opportunities to run out."

I hung up and sat thinking about the long day – the grief and frustration it had brought. We were like foot-soldiers without a leader. Our spirited objection to Payne's complacent stubbornness was in danger of waning. It's difficult to maintain an unpopular position if the only evidence for your argument is, "We know he wouldn't do this." As in, "I know my Johnny wouldn't hit another kid."

At that very moment, as if directed by the gods, my phone rang again. This time it was Coop.

"I just told Aunt Kirby about all we know. She grumbled that Payne was known to be short on bandwidth. She wants us to all get together tomorrow evening at her house and plan how we can bring about a full investigation."

Just like that, I was no longer moribund. I heard the bugle call. The troops were marching again.

"What time?"

"Six."

"I went around to the Sheriff's Office to talk to Sheriff Davis, but he's away in Europe on vacation."

"Yeah, I know. Kirby knew about it."

"See you in the morning."

"See you."

# 6

I checked the Weather Underground before setting off for breakfast. A four-day stretch of sunny skies was the upbeat forecast. The ride into Lake Leelanau was a breeze until I shifted into the top gear for the downhill mile into town. The derailleur carried the chain too far and right off the sprocket. I coasted to N.J.'s and got off. It was a short uphill push to Caballo Bayo. I'd get napkins there for the greasy repositioning of the chain. I could adjust the gear shift myself, but the whole bike deserved a tune up from the guys in Suttons Bay.

I was last to arrive. Coop was saying . . .

"Carla has a cousin who's a deputy. Maybe he has some influence with Payne. We'd have to approach him through Carla."

"I know a bit about how helpful Carla would be," N.C. said. "When I took Oscar back there yesterday, I moved the conversation toward the question of what Fuss would have been doing on the boat. It was quickly apparent she had no doubts about Payne's reading of the event. I threw in a mild question like, 'Do you remember your dad ever going fishing alone?' She said, 'No', but there was no flicker of a sign that this bothered her. I also got the impression – just a feeling – that she didn't welcome any questioning. Didn't want any complications - death by accident was easier to deal with.

"That eliminates any help from her," Coop agreed.

"Also, and it's very interesting. Vince was - now keep in mind that this was only a few hours after he'd heard from the police of Fuss's death – he was on the phone and what I could make out from his side of the conversation, he was talking to someone – a builder, I'd guess, about upgrading the kitchen in Fuss's house. He was very excited. Why upgrade the kitchen? Is he thinking about selling the house – only hours after learning it would be his?

"And as I left, I said again how sorry I was, and that I would see him at the funeral. For a moment he didn't seem to know what I was taking about then said, "Oh, oh yeah."

After N.C.'s report, there were long silences as we ate.

N.C. laughed out loud. "It's just unbelievable that Fuss without telling anyone of his plans would go out in that boat without Oscar to fish all alone!"

Now you might wonder why we were finding it so difficult to accept the fishing version of Fuss's behavior. That a person might decide to do something different for a change – out of line with their usual pattern – may

51

warrant one's notice, one's surprise even, but weren't my friends and I going a bit overboard in our reaction? Maybe you think our feelings were hurt, because he stood us up and did his own thing rather than treating our silly betting ritual with the seriousness we demanded. Hey, I can see how you might think that . . . unless you knew Fuss Quarrals. I have never known anyone – we four have never known anyone – you have never known anyone whose habits were as unwavering as his. A small for instance: every morning he would greet me with "And what does the day have in store for you, Al?" And when breakfast was over, he'd leave saying, "C'mon, Oscar, the world awaits us." Same words every time. He was such a good-hearted guy that we accepted his rigidity as an endearment.

"It's crazy-making!" I asserted.

"Amen," intoned N.C.

"Leave it, we'll work on it tonight," said Coop.

We searched for other subjects. First, it was Itch's displeasure with his breakfast.

"He goes for months eating and enjoying the same thing and then one day he acts like I'm trying to poison him."

"Contrary to popular belief, dogs are mysterious," Coop said. "We like to think their only objective in life is pleasing us humans. Then they slip up and reveal mysterious hidden agendas."

"I have no such illusions about Kato," I put in. "He has never tried to even appear to please me."

Next, Sam complained that Natalie had described him as "jowly."

Coop patted Sam on the shoulder and reassured him, "I've heard it said that 'jowliness' is in the eye of the beholder."

Sam thought about this and began slowly nodding. "Yes, There's truth there. Natalie recently went on a diet that involves starving herself twelve hours a day."

We left Caballo Bayo saying we'd meet at six that evening.

I'd grabbed a fistful of paper napkins for repositioning my bicycle chain, and now made the adjustment and pedaled off.

Arriving home, I decided to drive to Leland to return an overdue book to the Leland Library.

Since the time of the ancient Greeks, libraries have been experienced as sanctuaries of peace and rationality—repositories of wisdom. Today, however, most popular novels deal with tales of horror, murder, emotional and psychic pain, drugs and duplicity. OK, the Greeks had that covered too.

The Leland Township Library, tucked into an elbow of the Carp River that flows through the center of town, is a gem of small-town libraries. Lots of light through the large windows and comfortable furnishings made for an enjoyable visit in any season The staff, professionals and volunteers, were clearly happy to be there with you.

I laid my book on the return table and waited for Jake, the Assistant Director to be free.

"Keep batting one thousand and recommend the next one," I challenged when he came over.

"*The True Deceiver* by Tove Jannson."

"Sounds like it's about a confidence man?" I wondered aloud.

He only smiled and consulted the computer on the desk in front of him.

"MEL has it." He began filling out the request for me. MEL is short for Michigan Electronic Library which links all the state's public libraries and is a great asset for all library users.

"You're sure now?" I challenged.

"Would I risk a perfect batting average?"

I left my car at the library, cut through the grounds of the Old Art Building and walked the two blocks to Fishtown, my destination for lunch. There is no traffic light at the main intersection in Leland and the cross-walks on a summer weekend feature a steady stream of pedestrians. Driving through town is an exercise in patience. Just when the crosswalk clears and you touch the accelerator, a baby stroller ventures forth from the other corner. By the time the stroller is safely across, a new cohort of sightseers has entered the crosswalk from the other direction. It felt good, now, being on foot and the one stopping the traffic for a change.

Fishtown was the historic center of Leland's once thriving fishing industry, now only represented by Carlson's Fishery, which continues selling great whitefish. The rest of the quaint old buildings have morphed into various enticements for the tourist dollar. One of the shanties made sandwiches. At least a couple of times a summer I buy one and eat it sitting at one of the picnic tables that overlook the harbor. I was early so the line extended only a few yards outside the door.

When standing in a line without a companion, I, like most, have the ability to retreat within my own thoughts while still leaving a tiny part of my brain in the line to cause my feet to shuffle forward as required. I was pursuing the important question of where I might have put my conduit pipe cutter, or to whom I might have lent it, when a voice at my elbow said, "Penny for your thoughts."

Emerging from thoughts about an evasive tool, I found myself looking at an attractive female face. Without a fully engaged brain, I attempted to say, "Beth." The "th" came out barely audible, because I was addressing, after all, the former UN Ambassador again.

"Not too bad," she said playfully. "Now try again with more emphasis on the final fricative. BeTH."

I smiled with appreciation for this like-minded creature. "Good morning, Beth. Are you sightseeing, or have you perhaps come to buy a fish?"

"Ah yes, I was tempted to buy a fish at Carlson's, but then I wouldn't know what to do with it. I can't just hand it to my friend Carole and say, 'Cook this for me.'"

"Why not? I'll bet she has half-a-dozen whitefish recipes and the ingredients to go with them – we all do here."

"Is that an offer to cook my fish?"

That caught me off balance. "Ah . . . certainly."

"Just kidding. We had whitefish last night; I think she said Blue Bird style. I'm just being a tourist down here this morning. I'm impressed with the way the character of Fishtown has been preserved. It's true it's now a retail outlet like a mall, but to me I see the pride of the community standing guard like a mother hen."

"Well observed."

"And you are standing in line to buy what? – a sandwich?"

"Yeah, I like to eat at one of the picnic tables over there," I said, pointing across the parking area to a hill. "Any plans for lunch?"

"Is that an invitation?"

"You're quick."

"At times."

"Great, I'll get the sandwiches and drinks, while you finish your tour."

"They're probably of a generous size, right? – sandwiches."

"Yeah, they are."

"I couldn't eat a whole one."

"Neither can I - let's split one."

"Perfect. You pick. I eat anything except sea urchin. Something diet to drink."

I stood smiling, watching her walk away toward the other shanties. She was perhaps the easiest person to relate to I'd ever met. Her easy assumption of intimacy had me scrambling to meet it. The line now seemed to be moving faster too.

She arrived back with perfect timing to carry her drink, and we walked to the tables on the hill overlooking the harbor. I'd bought what they called, "the Greek,' which I divided. We sat side-by-side facing the marina.

"Carole told me about the subscription film program that she and you and your other friends have been running at that small movie theater in Suttons Bay. It sounded like you all enjoy the time you spend doing it."

"Yes, we have. It's still the only place in this part of the state where one can see on a big screen the kind of film we've been showing."

"What's playing now?"

"Oh, it doesn't run in the summer. People have too many other things to do with summer evenings. We'll be getting together now to pick the films we'll show next year – any suggestions?"

"I'm afraid not. I'm not in the film avant-garde.

I'm always trying to catch up on films I've missed."

We concentrated on our sandwiches for a bit. She looked out on the marina scene before us.

"I deduce you're not a boat owner, Al."

"Deduce – detective work. Let's see . . . If I'd had a boat, I would have suggested we go aboard to have our sandwich." I looked at her for confirmation

She nodded.

"If I had a boat, I wouldn't sit here looking at the activity in the harbor, I would want to be a part of it."

She smiled and nodded.

"If I owned a boat, I would exude an aura of confident boat-owner belongingness."

We both laughed.

"Just kidding," I said. "Many of my friends are boat owners and I once had a sailboat."

"What happened?"

"The wind was too unreliable."

"A power boat then."

"B-o-o-r-i-n-g."

"An off-shore racer."

"Good for one teeth-rattling ride."

"In short, you're saving yourself a lot of money. How do you spend it?"

I held up my sandwich.

"You're holding out on me. You're not fat enough for that to be the answer."

"And what do you spend your money on?"

"My four grand-daughters."

"Lucky kids."

"They're at an expensive stage and their parents aren't big earners."

"I understand, what with absurd tuitions today.

It's an age that cleans out bank accounts."

She smiled and then retreated for the moment into her own thoughts.

"Penny for your thoughts."

"Sorry, I was just thinking of the four rascals."

"Rascals are they?"

"Yes, all different, as if you had written them roles in something like Little Women."

"Do you get to see them often?"

"Yes, fortunately. Both my sons and their families live near me in Boston. I'll see them day after tomorrow."

"You're leaving so soon?"

"Yes, but I'll leave with fond memories of this place."

Here, I can only express my reaction in retrospect. The multiple thoughts and feelings I had were condensed beyond identifying them individually at the time, like those encrypted messages that are transmitted in a millisecond but print out as dozens of pages of text. I had strong feelings about Bethany Parker, but I could not – dared not let them advance beyond the unspoken. Could not, because my perception of her, my emotional experiencing of her was occurring faster than I'd been required to identify for years. Dared not, because "sound" judgment warned me I was too old to have any notions in the direction my feelings were pointing. She had talked of her family and of the profound part it played in her life. And she had included the fact that she would, "leave the day after tomorrow." I knew what she was saying, and my "sound" judgment agreed – we were ships passing in the night.

"I'm sure everyone here is happy that you decided to come. I know I am."

We finished the lunch and talked on for a while.

"A part of my mission in town today is to do some shopping for Carole. I'd better be on my way." She gave me a very friendly smile and said, "Thanks for lunch."

We exchanged phone numbers as people do doubting at the same time that they'd ever call.

"I'll walk with you to the Merc."

On the sidewalk in front of the store I felt an urge to say something else—to hold on to her a little longer. Perhaps what I said was stupid, but it was all that came to mind.

"Do you think we'll ever have a world government? I mean one with teeth that can prevent crazy dictators from grabbing power . . . prevent wars?"

With one hand holding the Merc's door open, she touched my arm with the other.

"You *are* a dreamer aren't you?"

# 7

Nearing home, I passed the mail lady's car with its red flag coming in my direction. The mail had been delivered. I crossed lanes pulled in close to my box and extracted a few letters and this week's *Enterprise.* This maneuver – facing oncoming traffic on the shoulder - was probably illegal, but the alternative would mean parking and walking across the road in rain and snow and possibly hail. So . . .

Inside my house, I checked Kato's water and then made coffee. I took a fresh cup onto my deck with the paper. I was surprised to see a letter in this edition from Fuss. I shouldn't have been. Like I said, he was constantly engaged with his adversaries, but his words today made it seem as if he were still alive.

*To the Editor:*
*You liberal jerks are hopeless. You think of im-*

migration like you think of eating plenty of vegetables (another liberal fad) If a little is good for you, then more is better and limitless vegetable eating is best of all. You refuse to see what is in front of your eyes: if you add one fruit after another to a cherry pie, soon it is no longer a cherry pie at all. The real America, the genuine America is like the one when the Declaration of Independence was signed.

James Winslow
Omena


To the Editor:

I love Mr. Winslow's analogy of America as a cherry pie. I'd like to remind him that if it were not for immigrants there would be no cherries for his pie. Who after all has picked those cherries for his pies all these years?

Frank Quarrals
Lake Leelanau


I smiled. So, these were Fuss's last published words. His opponents were going to miss him – as was the Editor.


The phone rang and I answered it.

N.C.'s voice. "How about my picking you up to go to Kirby's tonight?"

"Good. What time?"

"Say a quarter to six."


The mood was much different here on Kirby's deck than two nights ago. Through the silence, I could hear waves pushed by a south-west breeze breaking softly on the beach below us. Instead of a crowd of two hundred or so, there were only six: Kirby, N.C., Sam, Coop and his wife, Joan, and me. Ruth Ann had other plans for the evening. We sat around a table on the wide deck. We were all dressed casually, jeans and t-shirts for the guys. I did a double take on Sam's shirt. It was maize and blue with Michigan's seal on the front – University of Michigan. What was this? I knew he went to one of the Ivy Leagues . . . yes, Dartmouth. And then my eye caught a discord. It didn't say Michigan it said Michoacan, the University of Michoacan. I got his eye and pointed to his shirt.

"You caught me," I laughed.

"People see what they expect to see."

Kirby had discerned all the frustration our group was feeling when Coop called her after returning from the marina. This was her reason for convening this pow-wow. The stated reason for the meeting was to develop a strategy to encourage – to force – Payne into committing the Sheriff's Department to a full investigation into Fuss's death. I recognized in her demeanor as she greeted us, however, that she was also giving us an opportunity to vent our frustration. And the initial phase of the meeting was just that, each of us commenting on Payne's rudeness, pomposity, low wattage, pig-headedness, incompetence and pot belly.

She then summarized that from what we'd been saying it was clear that Payne was satisfied with only a superficial reading of the evidence.

"I did something on my own," she continued. "I thought I could solve the problem quickly and called the District Attorney, Matt Perkins. His mother, Maud, and I were best friends and when Maud visited me, Matt spent a lot of time playing with blocks on my kitchen floor. I figured Matt would extend credence to whatever my view was as a basic starting point. It didn't go as I'd expected. Almost immediately as I began to describe what had happened to Fuss, Matt interrupted me and said he'd already heard about the incident from Undersheriff Payne. Matter-of-factly he informed me it was clearly accidental death. A common case of an old person falling."

She sighed. "I saw that what I'd hoped for, a readiness to favor my point of view, because of my long friendship with his mother, or even a hearing where I'd be given the benefit of the doubt because of my seniority, was not to be. That advantage had probably expired at least a decade ago. Now he only saw me as an old person, one who adhered to outdated ways of thinking. I concluded I would have to use the approach I employ with people who are infected with some form of conspiracy. Never start by disagreeing with them head-on. This person has reached a conclusion that they are happy with, and he or she doesn't want to hear anything that upsets their peace of mind. So, one must appear to openly consider their idea, even though you think it's whacko. Consider their idea with interest – and you are not being dishonest, because you are very interested in how a seemingly normal person could hold on to such off-the-wall thinking."

That got laughs.

"I get them to fully state what they believe. Then, from that innocent stance I ask innocent questions – seeking to innocently understand fully. You are not satisfied with answers that don't adequately explain their position rationally and you ask for further clarification because you want to understand their point of view"

"Like, 'Do you mean' type of question?" asked Sam.

'Yes, and once you get them to seriously try to back their position with hard facts, your work is almost done. The unquestioned certainty they once had starts to become unglued."

"And they end up agreeing with you?" I asked.

"No, not always, but at least they end up feeling uncertain."

"And did this work with the D.A.?" asked N.C.

"Not a bit. He ended our conversation with, 'Nice to hear from you, Mrs. Spence. Have a good day.' There was a time when I had considerable influence here in the county. Today, my clout couldn't power a pen light. That doesn't matter. We can work together here this evening to put together our solid argument that will force this undersheriff to explain to us why a man would suddenly change life-long patterns and at the same time leave friends who were expecting him to take his part in an established custom without an explanation for his failure to show up. Failing that, we'll be prepared to present our doubts to Hoss Davis, when he returns. There is no doubt in my mind that he'll give us a fair hearing."

She looked around the table and seeing no disagreement, went on, "I'll take this down," she said with poised pen. "Now, what do we know to be the facts about Fuss's habits as it touches on the evidence in the case?"

There followed, in no orderly fashion, our sure knowledge of our friend and how this disagreed with Payne's point of view. Things we had all said before.

Joan Spence listened quietly to this with an inward smile, which escaped enough for me to catch it and identify it. I'm sure the smile meant she thought we guys were suffering from bruised feelings that a member of our exclusive club would betray the others and seek pleasure in a separate life. She knew better than to say this at this moment, but maybe she was a little – just a little – correct.

Coop got up to replenish our drinks.

Joan spoke, "It seems to me the argument we're making adds up to a list of 'nevers.' (At least she'd said "we.") Fuss would never do this or that. These 'nevers' have real substance to us, but they lack the force of hard evidence, such as, 1) man dead at foot of ladder of his boat. 2) Death caused by blow to head. 3) Blood on corner of table at the bottom of the ladder. 4) Fishing rods on deck. 4) Lunch box lying next to dead man. I'm afraid, friends, when Payne is challenged to explain his 'irrational point of view,' he'll have no need to look beyond the evidence he already has."

"Touche" said Kirby.

Before all the air went out of our balloon, I rushed in with what I thought was a patch.

"I was badly troubled when N.C. and I went to Fuss's house and found Oscar locked in the utility room. He had no food or water and he'd peed on the floor in one corner. All I could think of at the time was poor Oscar. But now, I see this as the kind of hard fact you're talking about, Joan. A dog that is your constant companion: walking, driving to the grocery, going out on the boat and so on, is never left behind without a good recognizable reason. Second fact: if the dog owner is going to do anything that might take longer than expected – possible engine trouble on the lake – he or she makes sure someone knows Fido is in the utility room and will need water and food and be let out to pee. This did not happen! Fuss loved Oscar! There is no way he would leave him unless he was certain he was taken care of. This is a fact as hard as the one's you listed."

Speaking in a conciliatory tone, Joan said, "You're right, of course, but it did happen."

"It did happen, yes, but Fuss would never have done it."

She wasn't going to go back and forth about that. Instead, she argued, "What if Fuss was only intending to take supplies to the boat and then come back to get Oscar?"

"Yeah, N.C. and I went over that possibility and rejected it. It just wouldn't make any sense to drive ten miles to Northport and back twice, when he could just have easily taken Oscar with him on the first trip."

"Then why didn't he?" she challenged.

Understand, I knew she wasn't being contrary in order to irritate. Joan wasn't like that. She was sincere now.

"He didn't because he wasn't going fishing."

"But Fuss did leave him in the utility room," she rebutted.

"Wrong! Fuss would never do that," N.C. emphatically stated as if each word were a rap of a judge's gavel.

"Then," Kirby reasoned in an even voice, attempting to return the mood to one of quiet discussion. "You're saying someone else left the dog there."

Silence followed until Sam, who hadn't contributed yet to the debate, put in, "Someone else means .

. ." He appeared to be doing a mental calculation. "It means another person was . . . hell, it was a setup. That means something stinks."

He looked around the group. "I can see it now – can't you? All of it was made to look like Fuss intended to go fishing and had an accident. Dirty dish to look like he had breakfast at home, fishing rod and lunch. Very convincing to anyone – but us. Failing to provide for Oscar was the only mistake."

Even after he had laid this out, I was slow to grasp the meaning.

"Why?" Joan asked. "Why go to all that trouble?"

The answer to her question would be obvious to anyone outside our group. The idea that anyone would want to hurt Fuss was an absurdity to us. He was probably the world's most inoffensive person, always ready with a helping hand for anyone. In fact, the idea was so repugnant none of us wanted to voice it.

Coop, the veteran reporter and facer-of-facts, put It In aseptic, objective terms. "In most cases, the intent of the kind of set-up you're suggesting – to make it look like an accident - is to cover-up for a . . . homicide."

A dense silence fell upon the scene. It was caused by the paralysis of each person's thinking apparatus. It was like walking off a cliff—no place to put your next step.

"Excuse me for saying so Coop," said N.C. "but that's as ridiculous as saying he was going fishing alone. Fuss was incapable of getting himself murdered."

In my mind, I seconded that.

"Still, if it quacks like a duck," Coop persisted.

Maybe her age had moved her out of a commanding position in county politics, but age had done nothing to blunt her inherent leadership ability. Kirby took over our rudderless group.

"Coop's entirely right," she instructed. "We are having difficulty getting our minds around the idea that anyone would want to kill Fuss, but a quack is a quack."

Sam emitted a burst of laughter. "I'm just imagining Payne holding his sides laughing, when we tell him we've figured out Fuss was murdered."

"Let's not give him that opportunity," Kirby said with a malicious smile. "We'll identify the murderer and drag him or her to jail hog-tied."

We were silent again as the meaning of what she'd just said sank in. We were going to investigate on our own. Make a citizen's arrest. She'd wasted no time. I looked around the group and discerned that the others needed more time.

Joan sensed the same. "Let's eat," she said, waving toward a table set with buffet fare she'd brought along consisting of Honey Baked Ham, potato salad and baguettes from Nine Bean Rows.

Filling my plate, settling into a chair, taking first bites and commenting on its tastiness was in the foreground, but trying to catch my balance mentally, because of the ground that had been covered so quickly was buzzing in the background. Fuss was murdered! We would catch the killer! It wasn't helping that I was being reminded of Andy Hardy and his friends putting on a show.

With a playful smile, N.C. teased, "Sam did his part, made us see this was a set-up for murder. Who'll take the first shot at naming the killer?"

Savoring her last spoonful of ice cream with Sand-er's hot fudge, Kirby thanked Joan for the meal, then said, "I'm afraid we'll be swamped with random ideas if we don't first have a structure from which to proceed. We'll need to be organized. Each will have tasks and the others will have to be kept up to date with each person's progress. So, to begin with, make sure you have everyone's cell number.

We had all streamed enough British detective series to know who the Detective Chief Inspector was here, so I said it, mild humor in my voice. "I nominate Kirby our DCI."

There followed, "I second" and "Hear, hear." All were serious.

"I accept." Her smile said, "I know there is the absurd about what we are undertaking but all the same we are going to do it.

"Let's see," she went on, "We should have a meeting place, which would also be a place to drop off stuff if there's a need."

"That would be Caballo Bayo," Sam said. "Jill would also take messages."

"She's the waitress at Caballo Bayo, correct?" Kirby asked. "And she'd be willing you think?"

"Definitely," I answered. "She liked Fuss very much. She'd be very willing to help."

Kirby nodded. "Since we have our whole team assembled, we should discuss our plan of action – decide how we should begin."

Standing up, Coop said, "The cops are usually drinking coffee from the department's machine. We don't have that, but I can get anyone another beer, wine, soft drink?"

Everyone passed.

"OK, let's begin," Kirby said, eager to move ahead. "As we've heard many times, a murderer must have motive, means and opportunity. Anyone who has at least one of those and, also has some relationship to the case is a suspect until proven otherwise."

That sounded good and very professional to me. I'd picked a good leader.

"Let's take motive first," she went on. "Who stands to gain by Fuss's death?"

"Carla," Sam said without hesitation.

"Yes, that's probably true," agreed Kirby. "Do we know anything about Fuss's will?"

No one responded.

"Sam, that's your assignment. Find out when it will be read and who benefits."

"Vince was talking to a builder about doing some remodeling of Fuss's house, when I went up there with Oscar," said N.C. "He must be pretty sure Carla will get the house. I wonder if it's remodel to sell."

"That was quick," I observed. "Your father-in-law isn't in his grave and you're already remodeling his house? In my opinion, that puts Vince ahead of Carla as a suspect."

"That reminds me," said N.C. "but maybe I'm getting ahead of the program. We're talking about motive."

"Our 'cop shop' is known for encouraging out-side-the-box thinking," Kirby said archly. "What came to mind, N.C.?"

"When Al and I went to Fuss's place looking for Oscar, we turned on the answering machine to _" He hesitated, realizing too late that he was confessing to listening to another person's private messages.

"Since we are a special branch of law enforcement," Kirby pronounced with authority, "we issue our own search warrants. What did the message say?"

"Yeah, of course. Ah, the message was from Vince saying he was sorry he had fouled up on the realty job Fuss had got for him and that he was going to Grand Rapids that night to close on a real estate deal he'd negotiated so he'd collect the commission and that he'd be back the next day. The recording was made – it seemed – the night Fuss disappeared, July 3$^{rd}$ and he said he'd be home on the 4$^{th}$. That means he was in Grand Rapids the night Fuss was killed."

"If he was in fact there," Sam said sarcastically.

"OK," Kirby said, "N.C., that's your job. Check on that alibi."

After a pause, Sam offered, "Fuss was always battling with some loonies in the *Enterprise*. I read some letters aimed at him that were as close to a threat as the paper could allow—maybe closer than it should have allowed."

That was a surprising thought. I could see what Sam meant. I'd never thought it amounted to more than spitball throwing, but on the other hand, one didn't really know how warped the mind was behind some of the paranoid ideas expressed.

I could see that it looked like a longshot to Kirby, but she shrugged. "Do some research, Sam. See if anyone stands out as a suspect. I don't want you to get in any trouble but check out the alibi of any hot prospect."

We six sat quietly now, stymied by Fuss's lack of enemies.

"Excellent," pronounced Kirby in an upbeat tone. "Let's move on to opportunity. What comes to mind?"

"That would depend on where it happened," I

said. "Can we narrow that down."

Coop took a shot. "The boat is the obvious place. But then there's Fuss's house. Oscar was locked in the utility room. Phony cereal bowl was there on the table."

"Fishing rods," N.C. came out with. "He kept them in the garage."

"If it happened at the house, then Fuss's car got to the marina some way," said Joan. "Maybe the car was used to take his body to the marina."

Out of the blue, a question came to my mind. "This is beside the point a bit, but Joan saying Fuss's car was used made me wonder how the murderer managed to leave the marina. This would be late at night, correct? If the person lived near Fuss, then how did he get back home? And if he lived near the marina and could walk home, how did he get to Fuss's in the first place? This would suggest there was an accomplice?"

"When Al and I were in Fuss's house to get Oscar, we, of course, were not looking for evidence of him being killed there," N.C. explained. "We've got to get back in the house and go over it carefully. I only wish we hadn't locked up the house and returned the key to Vince."

"No problem," I shot back. "I know where he hid a house key."

"As soon as you can," Kirby urged, "you two need to return there. If Vince is the killer, he would be certain to return as soon as possible to be sure he hasn't overlooked something."

"Thinking of opportunity, If Fuss was killed at the house, wouldn't that mean it was someone Fuss knew well enough to let him, or her in the house?" Coop looked around for confirmation of his deduction.

"I don't think that's true," Sam objected. "Fuss would have let anyone come in. 'Hello, my name is Joe Smith. I'd like to come in to a ask you a few questions.' 'Sure, Joe, c'mon in.'"

'So much for my brilliant idea."

"'Means' is the final member of the murder triad," said Kirby, moving ahead. "Your thoughts about that."

"I'd want to know what the head wound was like," Joan responded.

"Yeah, your generic 'blow to the head' could be delivered by anything, in which case everyone, except toddlers, might have the means," said Sam.

"I have an idea," offered Coop. The publisher of the *Enterprise* worked under me at the Chicago Tribune, when he started out as a reporter. We had a good relationship back then and are still friends. I don't want to ask him directly to find out the autopsy details for me, but if the subject just happened to come up in a conversation, I might be able to get an answer. It's about time I asked him to join me for a cup of coffee."

"Good." With the kind of gung-ho, locker room smile a coach might have before the big game, Kirby went on, "We've made a beginning on a proper investigation. We'll report all our findings to everyone on the team as soon as we learn anything and call another general meeting as needed. Anything else?"

"Don't you think the team should have a name," Joan said with a mischievous smile.

I think the suggestion was disingenuous, because knowing our group, she'd expect that we'd spend time now coming up with something like "Old Farts Murder Club", or "Edentulous Gumshoes."

Coop raised his hand for silence. "The name must

reflect the dignity of our purpose. The name shall be: 'Superannuated Sleuths of Leelanau County' or SSLC for short."

Kirby quickly said, "All in favor? The ayes have it! The SSLC is adjourned."

We all rose and headed for our cars. One thing about being old, you can pursue a serious goal without taking yourself too seriously.

# 8

Figuring Vince would not return to reassure himself he'd made no tell-tale mistake – if he were the killer – until after he and Carla had had breakfast, N.C. and I drove in my car to Fuss's house at 5:30 a.m.

I unwound the cord from the cleat that was fastened to a tree in Fuss's side yard, so I could lower the birdfeeder. Fixed to the inside of the lid was the hidden key to the front door.

I unlocked the door and stepped inside. N.C. stood outside on the doormat yawning.

"I'll bet you're the only person who has come through this door with his shirt tail out and his fly unzipped," I quipped.

"Close your eyes ladies."

We had no plan in mind for this inspection, but we both moved toward the utility room. We knew the killer had to have been there, since that's where he'd locked up Oscar. And in our minds now we were sure there was a killer. When we'd been in the room earlier our thoughts were totally on Oscar, now we stood and tried to critically observe everything around us. The first thing we both saw and remarked on at the same time was the wrench lying on the sink drainboard. I realized I'd noticed it and yet not noticed it when we were here before. It was what I always called a pipe wrench about a foot and a half long, the "Ridgid" brand name was on the shaft. The jaws were open a couple of inches.

"Nice weapon," N.C. said. "If we were cops, we'd send it for fingerprints."

"We could wrap it up and save it for evidence in case Payne considers murder."

"No good. It's already beyond evidence. We could be planting it here this morning."

N.C. picked it up. "The underside is a little damp. I believe this wrench may have been rinsed off. See here. Look, a thin coat of rust is forming."

He was right. N.C. then made a few chops in the air with the tool.

"I'm not an authority on blunt head injuries, but I think a single lick in the right place would be sufficient," he pronounced.

"What could Fuss have been using that for in this room?" I wondered out loud.

N.C. looked around the room and back at the sink. "Plumbing?"

He slowly and painfully sank down on one knee and peered under the sink. Reaching up underneath with the wrench, he tried the open jaws on the lock-nut. "Fits," he grunted and began crawling back out and standing with the help of a hand on the sink top.

"He must have had a leaky sink. See if the old gasket is in that trash can."

The plastic waste can was under the drainboard, so I pulled it out and there it was, a worn-looking rubber gasket.

"Well, my friend, what can we make of this?" N.C. charged.

"I can think of two 'nevers' off hand. One: Fuss would never fail to put a tool back in its proper place after using it. Two: he would never wash a tool off and leave it to air-dry."

N.C. nodded emphatically. "Lord I'd love to be able to do fingerprints."

"Yeah, and the cops could take that sink apart and test for blood. It looks like he was killed here in the utility room. I can't quite picture how that would be— Fuss killed while fixing a leaky sink?"

I got out my phone and took a picture of the wrench lying on the drain board and of the old sink washer, then said "Let's move on."

The cereal bowl and coffee cup were gone from the dining room table. The briefcase was in the same place. I trotted into the kitchen and opened the dishwasher. There were the bowl and cup.

"Carla must have been here," I ventured. "Vince would have left the bowl and cup on the table if he's the killer and had set up the 'breakfast at home before the fishing thing', and if he isn't the killer, he could care less about dirty dishes on the table."

"Bingo."

"We questioned the cereal bowl, because we've never seen Fuss eating cereal at Caballo Bayo. An essential question is, does he have any cereal in the house?"

My question sent us both looking through cupboards.

"Here's a box!" exclaimed N.C., holding up a box of Frosted Flakes, Tony the Tiger's big smile contrasting with N.C.'s frown.

"Frosted Flakes?" I had an idea. "What is the expiration date, or what does the 'better if used by' date say?"

N.C. held the box top toward the light. "'Best if used before 02 2005.' I'd say he's had these a while."

"Grandchildren. I'll bet he kept them on hand for his two grandchildren when they were kids."

N.C. peaked into the box. "Half full. Fuss all over. Don't waste anything."

"Do you think Fuss would eat Frosted Flakes that are fifteen years old? Say, if he was in a hurry to get on his way to his boat? Because, if the answer is even maybe, then the presence of the cereal bowl on the dining room table means zilch."

N.C. put the box back in the cupboard and stood and thought a moment. "See what you mean – yeah, it doesn't help us."

"Let's look in the other rooms."

N.C. led the way. The first room off the hallway from the kitchen was the bathroom I'd used many times, toilet with lavatory.

"He was hit on the head, so we're looking for blood spatter," N.C. said.

We concentrated, trying to sharpen our inspection beyond the normal cursory inventory of our surroundings. We got no reward; the room was devoid of the suspicious. The next room along the hall was Fuss's study. I'd given the room a cursory glance the first time we'd been here. Now, I viewed it more carefully. One could easily spend relaxed time here, the dimensions were pretty good for one person, not so small to be cramped, not too large to negate cozy. One easy chair with ottoman, one medium sized desk with leather cushioned swivel-chair. Behind the chair; bookshelves from floor to ceiling. On the desktop; phone, notepad and ballpoint, pictures of family – wife Claudia, Carla and two granddaughters. There was also a plaster-of-Paris cast of a frog that had once been green. Most likely a kindergarten gift from the granddaughter who was now a cardiology fellow at the Cleveland Clinic. There was also a letter opener. You don't see those much anymore. Setting aside those who must open a hundred business letters a day, the rest who get half-dozen letters be they love letters or bills, can be divided into two groups - the person who reaches for a letter opener and those who rip away. A member of the first group does most things properly throughout life. I'm a member of that second group. The letter opener itself was a work of art. Fashioned from a hard, dark wood, the handle was intricately carved. Asian I'd guess.

I opened the top drawer. Neatness was the first impression anyone would have. A large checkbook lay on the right side. To the left were two sizes of envelopes and two shallow boxes, pens in one, pencils in the other. I opened the checkbook and looked at the register. It looked like mine – checks to the gas and electric company, Herman Brothers' Lawn Care, and Chase Credit Card Service and for the expected amounts. Then there was recorded a check for twenty-four hundred dollars to "B Campbell." I wondered for a moment what that was for, before I turned the page, which repeated the same story of small amounts for household expenses. Then another check made out to B. Campbell. This time for twelve thousand, dated last year.

"That's a hefty amount," commented N.C. over my shoulder.

I turned the page and there was B Campbell again. This time for six thousand. This was the last page in the register. Where would the previous registers be?

"Maybe there's a filing cabinet." I wondered aloud.

N.C. walked over to a door we'd not opened earlier.

"Here we go."

I stood behind the desk and watched him. Here was a closet with shelves holding stationery, copy paper and a four-drawer filing cabinet. N.C. tried the top drawer. Contrary to Fuss's habit of not locking his car, the filing cabinet was locked.

N.C. observed, "A detective worth his salt would whip out a lock pick and open this!"

"Huh, I wonder what that B Campbell business was all about?"

"Anything in the world. Maybe Fuss played online poker."

"With his actuarial skill, you could bet the money'd be traveling in the opposite direction. Anyway, nine chances in ten it's outside of our interest."

As N.C. stood at the filing cabinet, I'd been standing between the desk and bookshelves that covered the wall behind it. The books were so perfectly aligned Fuss must have used a surveyor's transit. All except one that stuck out a couple of inches from the rest. Absent mindedly, I tried to push it into alignment with the rest in the row. The book resisted my push enough that it drew my attention. It looked like a photo album. I pulled it out a little farther and confirmed that it was an album, then I pushed it back into the shelf and perfectly in line. Fuss would have appreciated that.

"A summary of our findings, my friend?" I asked as we were about to leave the study.

"Discounting the payment to 'B Campbell,' we found nothing, except that we can be sure nothing violent happened here in this room."

We moved on to Fuss's bedroom, where the red light was still flashing on the answering machine.

"Carla hasn't taken the messages off the machine," N.C. noted. "That's good. I need to listen to Vince's message again for the name of the motel he said he was staying at. I thought he'd said Starlight Motor Lodge, but there is no such place on Google. My memory is not only kaput, it makes up stuff on its own."

We listened to the messages again and heard Vince say he was staying at the Sunrise Motor Lodge.

"Sunrise damnit, not Starlight. Sunrise, Sunrise."

"Don't be hard on yourself," I said. "After all, they're related – sunrise, starlight."

"Don't say that; It will only confuse me."

As we turned to the rest of the house, I kept trying to crank up my acute observing powers, but they were lagging. That never seemed to happen to Sherlock or Harry Bosch. Two more bedrooms and another bath failed to yield any evidence of a malevolent intruder. In fact, the bedrooms looked like no human had ventured that far for a long time. I'm given to this kind of sentimental attribution of human feeling to inanimate things, the kind that now had the bedroom seem happy that someone had finally wandered this deep into the house.

"Al, Vince may be along any time now, we'd better 'amscray,' as the kids say."

"N.C., kids haven't said 'amscray' for a long, long time."

"That right? How 'bout 'we better haul ass.'"

"Now I hear you."

I locked the front door and put the key back on the bird feeder and hoisted it into position.

# 9

We got back in the car and headed for breakfast at Caballo Bayo.

"Did you think we moved our project forward?" I asked.

"If the project is finding evidence that would convince the police Fuss was murdered, the answer is, no. However, if the wound on Fuss's head could be made by that wrench, the answer is, yes. Definitely. That wrench was heavy enough to cause a skull fracture if given a good swing. The significant thing is that it was on the sink. After using it, Fuss would have put it back where it was kept before he did anything else."

"Right. That is, if he had a chance to do anything else. Fuss's chances to do anything may have ended right there."

"Say, Al, drop me off at home. I'd like to get Itch

and walk to breakfast with him,"

The inside lights were just being turned on at the café as I drove up and parked. I sat for a couple of minutes more to give Jill some time, then went inside and told her of the meeting we'd had the night before and of the decision to undertake an investigation on our own. She was excited by the designation of Caballo Bayo as headquarters and her as dispatcher. She seemed to have recovered from the heartbreak over her boyfriend. I left her smiling and starting the coffee machine, as I headed for the john. When I came out, N.C. had arrived, so I went outside to my stool at the counter. Itch had already settled down beside N.C.'s stool for his usual nap. He opened one eye and raised an eyebrow as I sat down.

N.C. had doodled "SSLC" in various scripts on a paper napkin. He used to do lettering on hotrods for pocket change back in his misspent youth, so he was damn good.

Jill, her curiosity getting the better of her, leaned over the counter and tried to see what he was doing. He immediately covered the napkin with his hand.

Laughing, she asked, "What in the world are you writing, N.C.?"

"You don't wanna know, Jill. If I showed you, then I'd have to kill you."

With my hand shielding my mouth, as if whispering a secret, I informed her, "He belongs to a secret force doing good in the world. After dark he goes out wearing a costume."

She shielded her mouth toward me and said, "You mean like Batman?"

"Exactly. Only he looks more like a chicken."

She was saved from the awful contemplation of N.C. in a chicken suit, by two customers coming in the front door of the café.

Sam now appeared wearing an apricot-colored outfit including the shoes. I knew he didn't buy these ensembles – at least I hoped it was Natalie's doing, but he did have the nerve to wear them. Was I jealous of his bling? Yes, to be honest. I'm a guy with no flair.

A sarcastic comment on his attire was forming, which I rerouted into, "So today, my friend, you're descending into the murky waters of "Letters-to-the Editor'."

"Yeah, I'll stop at the *Enterprise* first to see how easily I can access their archives. If that's not an option, I'll head to the library and read all the issues they have on hand."

"I wonder how many letters the editor rejects, because of unprintable extremes of one kind and another. They must save them all for legal purposes. Or would they? Supposing some guy did threaten to kill his pen pal: would the paper send that along to the sheriff? And how direct would the threat have to be? How about, 'Maybe your wife will miss you this Christmas.' Or 'If I were you, I wouldn't bother making your next car payment.' And, who determines the seriousness of a threat? The editor? A panel of psychiatrists, a panel of lawyers? I know I don't envy them."

"I hadn't imagined it being so complicated," Sam said.

"I heard a guy say once that everything is complicated. The only thing that's not complicated is our wish for things to be uncomplicated."

"If I could get hold of those rejected letters, that

would be a shortcut to the real loonies," Sam mulled.

Coop had taken a seat at the counter as Sam said this.

"You're right, Sam," Coop agreed, "but I'm sure the last thing the paper would be willing to share with you are those rejected letters. On the other hand," Here, Coop made a gesture toward Sam's apricot duds. "If the person you talk to is a *Vogue* subscriber, you might get lucky."

"Jealousy is easy to spot," Sam observed blandly. He leaned back and made as if he were sizing Coop up. Nodding he said, "No question, Natalie could do a lot for you."

N.C. changed the direction. "Wasn't it great the way Kirby Spence took charge last night? The worst mess imaginable is a committee made up of a bunch of disoriented old guys."

"Ah but, that's only true if the group members are happy with the commander. If not, that's another kind of a mess," I said. "Happily, I think we'd willingly follow Kirby's command to charge into enemy cannons."

"I've got to admit I feel discomfort about the duplicity I must stoop to in order to lead the *Enterprise* Editor into talking about the autopsy," Coop confided.

"You'll get over it." N.C. said. "You'll only be misrepresenting your motive for getting him to say more than he should. That must be standard operating practice for a journalist. Don't let the senator know you're interested in how he padded his expenses on his recent "fact-finding trip"—get him talking about foreign food, segue to restaurants, then mention a Michelin two-star you'd eaten in. He forgets himself and begins describing all the three-star places he'd sampled on the government tab and the premier grand cru wines he'd guz-zled."

"Thank you, N.C. I feel better already, being re-minded that I've escaped my two-faced professional life. But in retirement, aren't we supposed to be freed from life's ugly realities and hence able to assume our true honest and virtuous selves?"

"And you will, you will – right after you get the dope on the autopsy. As for myself, Kirby gave me the assignment of checking on the validity of Vince's alibi. Was he or was he not in Grand Rapids? I've got to drive down there to check it out. First, I'm paying a visit to the Gardner Realty in Suttons Bay to learn what I can about the sales contract Vince claimed was taking him to Grand Rapids."

"Sounds like a long day," I said.

"Yeah, but Itch is good company."

So, everyone had a definite task to work on— except me. A thought had been hanging around in my mind ever since the four of us had stood watching the police take Fuss from his boat, and that was that I'd like to get a look inside the boat. It had been impossible at that time, of course, but I was still drawn to going back and nosing around. Why not now?

"I'm going up to Northport to look around the boat. Maybe I can even get inside," I announced.

"That could only happen," N.C. predicted, "if you're there in the moment between padlocks – after the cops remove theirs and Vince attaches his,"

"Right, and if Vince is the killer, you better be-lieve he'll leave it open for as short a time as possible," Coop added the obvious.

"You're telling me I'd better get moving. Right!

Here I go."

Their analysis of the time factor had my heart racing. I hurried to my car, planning to take Eagle Highway from Lake Leelanau north to M22 – maybe ten minutes faster than going through Suttons Bay . . . only to find that the Road Commission was spreading loose gravel over fresh tar on this shortcut. A U-turn brought me back to my starting place and the need to take the longer route. Longer and slower. No passing, because perhaps eighty-five percent of the roads featured a double yellow line due to the many hills and curves in the county. That was usually OK with me; most of the time I was in no hurry. Right now, I was behind a car driving forty. Having to slow down allowed a fact to elbow its way through my annoyance. Payne considered Fuss's death to be an accident. The body had been discovered two days ago. How likely was it that he'd keep the boat padlocked this long? Not very. He'd have turned it over to Carla by now and Vince would have locked it up. There was no reason to rush! My autonomic nervous system throttled back, sending a critical message to my cerebral cortex, "Slow down! No more panic! Take it easy." I, now, enjoyed the drive up the shore of the bay.

I parked in the small lot at the south end of the marina where Fuss's Jeep had been parked. I got out and tried to imagine the situation a killer would have faced. It was obvious why the guy would park here, darker and perhaps a few steps closer to pier "B" than the main lot at the other end of the marina. Still, it was farther than I would care to have carried Fuss's body. Fuss had been lightly built but would be long and very floppy when dead. Ideally, one would like to force the victim to walk to the boat at gun point, then hit him on the head. If he'd been killed at home with that wrench, then carrying him to the boat would be a bitch. I know I'd need help, so an accomplice was a good possibility. The killer could transport the body here in the Jeep and leave with the accomplice in another car.

I walked slowly along the sidewalk to pier "B" scanning the lawn that extended away from the docks. After all, the cops had had no reason to search the area, so maybe there was a clue here where the killer had to carry Fuss's body. I can now attest to the fact that the marina and the adjacent picnic area is well maintained. Aside from a Hacker-Pschorr bottle cap hiding under a clover leaf, I found nothing; no handkerchief with em-broidered initials, no cigarette butt marked with a cus-tom-made shade of lipstick, I only found evidence of some boat owner's wish to impress his guests with an over-priced imported beer.

I walked out onto pier "B" to the fourth slip. Fuss's boat floated quietly, like an old dog waiting loyally for his master to return. My eyes immediately went cabin hatch door. A padlock was visible. The question was, whose? I climbed from the dock into the boat cock-pit and examined the lock and read, "Property of the Leelanau County Sheriff's Department." "Well. I'll be damned," I said aloud. I couldn't get into the boat, but neither had Vince.

The cabin had four windows that rose about a foot above the narrow deck running around each side of the cabin. To look through them meant kneeling on the deck—not a configuration my body would accept - not if I wanted to stand again. I was determined to see inside, which meant lying on my abdomen and lifting myself on my elbows a few inches in order to peer into the dark interior. So be it; I yearned to see inside. The glare on the window was enough that I had to shield my eyes with one hand, leaving the body lifting to a single arm. In a short time, I was reduced to quarter minute periods of viewing. I managed this procedure at three windows while seeing nothing of interest. I lowered my head on my arm and felt . . . old. Then my memory of Kirby telling us to, "get out there and kick butt" recharged my resolve. I remembered what a professional photographer once told me when I complained about getting unwanted garbage cans and telephone poles in my pictures. He said to first look at the whole image in the viewfinder before focusing on the point of interest. Start at the top left-hand corner and scan back and forth letting yourself identify everything in the viewfinder. Then, adjust the angle and so forth until you've got the composition you want and, Snap. I crawled aft to the fourth window and began this systematic viewing with a mandatory rest for arms and back. I noticed the door to the head was open a crack and through the crack, I saw part of a small cooler. Now I remembered the harbormaster telling us that when he'd gone on board and discovered Fuss, there was also a small cooler on the floor of the cabin.

I rolled onto my back and lay thinking about the meaning of this. Maybe the sheriff's guys just picked the cooler up and placed it on the counter in the head and thought no more about it. If so, it could contain items of a phony lunch, things Fuss never ate, for instance. I had to look inside that box before Vince got hold of it! I'd have to get Payne to take possession of it! Make him listen to me.

I was excited by my discovery, but equally frustrated. I struggled stiffly to get up with a plan to call Kirby to have her call the District Attorney and get him to agree that I'd found real evidence and step in and protect it. I looked along the pier and what I saw was too good to be true – a sheriff's deputy probably coming to remove the padlock. I hurriedly scrambled back into the cockpit. He was not one of the deputies who'd been with Payne the other day. Maybe he was open to rational argument.

"You're an answer to my prayers, officer," I said in my friendliest voice. I went right on, "I'm Al Burke, a friend of the man who owned this boat. I left my reading glasses in the cabin the last time I went out with Mr. Quarrals and I haven't been able to get them, because of the padlock."

"That right? I'm Deputy Richards, I'm here to take the lock off, but I was told that the man's son-in-law is coming to put a new lock on. I don't know if I should let anyone in the cabin until . . ."

"Yes, Vince," I hurried to say. "I don't need to wait for him. It'll only take me a few seconds to retrieve my glasses."

No doubt Vince had been notified of the lock's immanent removal and the deputy would think it OK to leave the boat open. He'd be uncomfortable, however, walking away while I was inside the boat.

The deputy came onto the boat and began sorting through a ring of keys. "Yeah, I'm sure there's no problem. Run down and get your glasses and I'll wait for you."

He took off the padlock and slid the hatch cover open. I began to carefully descend the companionway ladder. In my eagerness to examine this suspicious cooler, I'd only been thinking of getting my hands on it. Another matter now occurred to me. If I found that the box did contain food not to be found in Fuss's house, in other words, a faked lunch and hence evidence of a faked accident, how could I prove what I'd discovered? I could have planted the bogus lunch myself! I thought of taking a picture of the cooler unopened and then another of it newly opened. I had my phone with me. But wait - what would that prove?

I called up to the deputy, "Officer, would you come down here a moment?"

He came down the steps backwards and then faced me. "Find your glasses?"

"Yes, thanks, but there is something else I noticed that may be important."

I opened the door to the head fully and pointed to the cooler.

"Some people I've heard are having strong doubts that Frank Quarrals's death was an accident. They're saying he was murdered – hit on the head. Then the killer tried to make it look like Frank was going fishing and fell and hit his head."

I paused, aware of a change in his attitude toward me – wariness.

"Anyway, that's what they're saying. So accordingly, Fuss, that is Frank, would not have really prepared a lunch. Any lunch in the boat would be a plant. You follow me?"

His eyes said he wished I was saying all this to someone else, but he wasn't reaching for his handcuffs - yet.

"Here's the thing." I went on hurriedly, "We've got this cooler here. It's most likely empty. The first of your guys who were here probably threw whatever was inside into the marina's garbage. No sense in letting things rot and cause a bad stink. Right? But, if there happens to still be food inside, then this new investigation I mentioned will demand to know exactly what it is."

"This new investigation," only existed in the minds of half-a-dozen septua and octogenarians but I thought I wouldn't be that accurate. All through my oration I was trying to judge on what side he would come down. Of course, he didn't want to make a mistake that would reflect badly on him. No one wanted that. The question was always how secure a person felt within themselves. Do you dare, in the moment, to do what you think is right, or must you do what you're sure some other party will think is right?

"For instance," I babbled on, "If Mr. Quarrals was a vegan and the lunch contains sausage sandwiches."

"You need a witness to the fact that you didn't plant sausage sandwiches in the box."

"Exactly." I said with relief. "That's it exactly."

He went into the head and was about to grasp the box's handle when he paused and reached into a rear pants pocket and came out with a pair of rubber gloves. Fantastic! He was open to finding evidence.

He brought the cooler out and placed it on the small table, the table Fuss was supposed to have hit his head on. He undid the latch and started to open the box. My heart stood still. I was like a contestant on a quiz show watching as the gift box he'd chosen blindly was opened by the gorgeous blond. Would it be a lump of coal or a new Lamborghini (a curse when insurance and maintenance were considered).

We were both now looking at a sandwich in a baggie and a pear.

The aroma of the pear having been confined in the box for several hot days now filled the cabin. The edge of the sandwich seemed to show something like salami. I began to reach for the baggie.

"No, no, no," he instructed. "Tampering with evidence."

"Right, right, right," I agreed but my heart was singing. Fuss never, never, never ate pears. He said the small grainy bits got under his denture. AND the deputy had referred to the cooler as evidence. This was big.

"What about the sandwich?" I prompted.

"Rather not touch it."

"Yes, of course – fingerprints."

I took out my phone and took a series of shots. Then it came to mind that Vince might arrive any second to take possession of the boat.

"This is solid proof that the lunch is phony. All Fuss Quarrals' friends know he never ate pears. He claimed they caused problems with his dentures. Maybe, you'd better secure this evidence. You know, take possession of it for the Sheriff's Office – put it in your patrol car."

He thought a moment, then took out his phone. "Jennie, this is Walt. I'm at the Northport marina where I just took the padlock off the Quarrals boat. There's gentleman here, Mr. Burke. He says an investigation into Frank Quarrals death has begun and that . . . Oh, OK . . . Yes, sir. This is Walt Richards. I'm at the boat . . . I see. I understand. There is a small cooler here in the boat . . . OK, roger that."

He put away the phone and turned to me. "It

seems there is no investigation. I was told the cooler belongs to the new owner and stays on the boat."

I'm sure Payne hadn't phrased it as benignly as Richards had just summarized. I knew it was pointless to protest. At that moment, I heard the tread of footsteps in the cockpit and then Vince shouting down into the cabin.

"Who's down there?"

"Yes," Richards answered, looking up the companionway. "I'm Sheriff's Deputy Richards. I just took our padlock off and a friend of Mr. Quarrals is here, because he had left his glasses on board the boat and wanted to retrieve them."

Vince said nothing as we made our way up the ladder. His expression was that of a guy who had just discovered two neighbors rummaging through his garbage can—irritated but unable to voice it.

"Did you find your glasses?" he asked sarcastically with a knowing smirk that said I was lying.

I pulled them out of my pants pocket (where I always keep them.) "Yes, thank you."

In my pocket was my camera with the picture of the pear and a white-bread sandwich with some variety of deli meat, which Deputy Richards would have to admit under oath was in a cooler aboard Fuss's boat. All Fuss's friends and relatives would swear he never ate pears. A worthwhile morning's work!

# 10

I drove back to the squad room AKA Caballo Bayo Café and went inside and asked Jill for a coffee and told her I had some new information to tell her when she had a moment. I then composed an email briefly describing the marina adventure and sent it off to the group. As I wrote I became acutely aware that any value the sandwich had for us hinged on whether Fuss had had any white bread or deli meat in his house. I'd taken a picture of the interior of the refrigerator, but I couldn't swear we'd looked through the drawers carefully. I needed to do that immediately! I needed to take pictures to prove there was no white bread or pears in Fuss's house. I started to get up, then sank back down in the chair. What a dumb idea! As if a picture of what wasn't there proved anything. A good lawyer would point out that Fuss could have used his last pear and the last of the white bread to make the sandwich. Still, I had the photos I'd taken on the boat. I checked the time on the wall clock and thought N.C. may have had time to drive to Grand Rapids. I called and he answered immediately.

"I'm gaining a greater respect for private detectives," he said. "The guys in the TV series say, 'I'm a private investigator,' and hotel clerks start babbling. Not so in real life. In real life they come back with, 'So what?' Real money must cross palms in the real world. I was sent on this mission underfunded."

"I'm playing a sad tune on my violin."

"Just sayin'. OK, what my twenty bucks bought was confirmation that Vince did register here at 5:30 on July 3rd. He paid for the room when he arrived. The clerk didn't see him go into the room nor did he see him again or notice whether his car was here during the night. It was a full house and so was the parking lot. So, Vince really has no alibi. He could have driven back to Fuss's house in three hours and done the deed. Plus, Gardiner, his former boss at the realty firm told me that the idea of closing a deal on the 4th and collecting a commission was hogwash. Simply put, Vince did not come down here for the reason he gave on Fuss's answering machine. We could learn a lot if we had access to his phone records. I don't have enough in the bank to bribe the right person at the phone company."

I digested what he'd related. I had nothing to suggest.

"What are your plans?"

"I'm coming back. I can't think how I can learn anything else here. I'll send a group email first to let the others know what I've just told you."

"Sounds good. See you in the morning."

Jill came finally and sat down at the table. I repeated what I'd put in the email to my fellow detectives and maybe too much of my frustration. She was upbeat about the photo of the sandwich and the pear and the deputy's certain confirmation.

So, I left Caballo Bayo in a good mood with the thought of dropping in on Sam. He lived a short distance away on Lake Leelanau Drive. As you make the turn off 204 is the sign that says, "The Village of Lake Leelanau Welcomes You." That should give one a smile – you're welcome here. Instead, it causes sadness in me when I think of the neat name the village used to have – Provmont. The name was inexplicably changed at a village council meeting in 1924. What a tragedy! Provmont carried intimations of elegance. Where are you from? PROV (soft French) mont. A whiff of perfume in a candlelit room. Or emphasizing "Mont." ProvMONT. Bold people in a brave new town. Make way for us! And the name is unique; even today Google can't find a cousin.

So, what could have happened at that village meeting back on that dark day in 1924? I imagined something like this. At these meetings someone has a burr under his or her saddle over some issue that the other members of the council don't care a damn about. You know what I'm talking about; you've been there. Now it so happened that this peninsula was settled by several ethnic groups maintaining distinct neighborhoods – farm neighborhoods, Polish, French, Norwegian and Bohemian. These areas roughly came together where the long lake which the Indians called Leelanau came to a central narrowing. Back in the nineteenth century, a village took shape there; it was named Provmont. Now as I picture this fateful council meeting in 1924, a Bohemian named Milo Housdek, let's say, who owned the rowboat livery and who was sick and tired of the French sound of the village name, took advantage of the fact that the two French descended members of the council were visiting a sick relative in Kingsley, to move to have the town's name changed to "Little Bohemia" (which wasn't all that bad) and would have been successful in passing his motion – since as I said before, the other members either 1) didn't give a damn 2) didn't understand the motion at all, or 3) needed Housdek to vote for a motion of their own. He would have been successful except for the late arrival of Lars and Olaf Carlsen who turned two thumbs way down. The crazy thing about situations like this is that once a change has been suggested, it seems a change must be made, even if the result is less desirable than what existed before the change. So, they struggled for a long time to agree on a new name until someone said, "I gotta get home to milk the cows. How about just naming the town after the lake and be done with it - Lake Leelanau?" What a shame! Try to imagine Chicago being renamed "Lake Michigan."

Sam lived about a mile south of Fuss's place. I just felt like talking to one of the guys and offloading more about what had happened at the marina. At the same time, I'd see if he'd collected any good candidates for the crazy-letter-writer theory. His car wasn't parked in front of the house, but unlike Fuss, he usually put the Audi Q8 in the garage. I walked to the front door and pressed the button. My eyes were drawn, as they were each time I approached the front door, to the unique glass door handle. Natalie had bought it in France, an antique made by Lalique, a famous glassmaker of the late nineteenth century. Sam had explained to us how it had cost "an arm and a leg" and not something which should be for general use as a working handle, but Natalie liked the idea of the Lalique handle being the first impression a visitor would have of her taste. I wasn't so sure. It seemed obvious to me that it had originally been intended as the handle to the boudoir of some French count's mistress. To open the door, one had to lay one's hand on the upper slope of a beautifully formed bare breast. Natalie's unalloyed, unapologetic exhibitionism was so honest and open that I simply had to smile. It was daunting for an upstanding mature gentleman like myself to reach out and grasp it. I forced myself. The door was locked . . . as I knew it would be.

I was smiling at my nonsense as I turned into my driveway. It wasn't until I made a cup of tea and sat with Kato on my back deck that I acknowledged what had prompted the silliness. It was my state of mind. I was thwarted, not a term I ever use, but it came to mind now and it fit. My friends and I were sure murder had been committed, but we couldn't prove it and the only suspect with a motive had an alibi. One, that while impossible to absolutely prove, was also impossible to disprove. The thing that had managed to seep through my gung-ho, we-can-do-it attitude, now, was a practical voice that said, "You're kidding yourself." Yes, Sam was still assessing possible letter-writing suspects, which was, let's face it, far-fetched. After that, we had nothing, and we would have to accept that and move on or make ourselves sick over it.

Aiding me in setting aside our obsession this afternoon was a home project. A couple of weeks ago N.C. had described the very large bobcat he had seen near his house. He was sure it was the size of a dog. With each repetition of the story, the cat got bigger until it was the size of a great Dane. He remained steady on one point; it could snatch up a cat like Kato on the dead run. I chuckled at his exaggeration but, it got me wondering what kind of critters wandered around my place after dark. So, I bought an inexpensive gadget online called "Blink" that would photograph and record the area behind my house. It was motion activated and would play back through my computer. The postman had delivered it this morning and that was my project for the afternoon. My mechanical skill confidence was average, but my electronic confidence was low. As it turned out the installation of the small camera on the side of my house was a snap. The computer part should have been, but it was prolonged by a misreading of the directions. Finally, I believed I had the thing working. I heated up ravioli I'd bought at Costco, and went to bed, saying good night to Kato who settled at the foot of the bed. It had been a long day.

Voila! It worked. In the morning, I opened the program on the computer and found that Kato and I had been visited by an opossum, its beady little eyes showing up as two bright spots. This was going to be fun – so long as a bobcat didn't crash the party - or a coyote.

I went into the bedroom to dress and took a moment to look out the window toward the pond. The sky was cloudless. A light breeze made cat's-paws of ripples on the pond's surface. The resident mallards were clearly invigorated judging by their quick little changes of direction as they swam.

After dressing I made sure Kato's bowl was full. He preferred, when the water wasn't frozen, to drink from a large metal dish outside, which required constant leaf removal. Maybe the leaves lent a special flavor like tea. I rolled the bike out of the garage and set off for Caballo Bayo.

I knew every pothole between home and breakfast. I also knew the two dogs. Around the second long curve lived a golden retriever I called "Happy Boy." He had to have remarkably sharp hearing, because he would come running out his driveway in time to meet me as I passed. His tail nearly wagged off and had what could only have been a smile on his face. His eyes said, "Good morning, Al, great to see you on the road again. Keep those wheels spinning!" I'd yell back, "Good Boy!"

The second canine was another matter, a mongrel from hell, a would-be autocrat, a dictator, a Heinrich Himmler wannabe. I had many names for him, which I won't go into. I think he lived at the road in wait for anything to come along that he could threaten. Once, I kicked out at his snapping teeth. That only pleased him. I considered carrying a can of pepper spray, but that would have put what should have been a pleasant ride into a whole new category. Instead, I followed advice my father gave me all those years ago: stand up to a bully! So, this one morning I slammed on my brakes jumped off the bike and rushed toward him shouting. Luckily, it worked, and he quickly retreated twenty yards before turning to tell me what he could have done to me if he'd wanted to. The thing is, he continues to do his empty boasting, but now from twenty yards away and I yell back, "Yeah, yeah, yeah."

As I coasted into the village, I noticed there was new construction beginning beside the post office. What was being built there? I cut off on the side street to the Bayo.

N.C. and Coop were there and Jill was busy with

the coffee ritual. We had never paid much attention to how our voices carried during our regular breakfasts. Being outside caused you to think you were no part of the restaurant. This morning, however, we spoke as if unseen diners within might be straining to hear.

Coop was the first to report on his contact with the publisher of the *Enterprise*.

"I hadn't had a one-on-one conversation with Jeff Wisdom for more than a year, so the first three-quarters of an hour was an enjoyable reminiscence with an old friend. Believe it or not he then brought up Fuss's death on his own, saying he thought he remembered my saying I was a friend of his. I said I had a lot of questions about Fuss's death, for instance did he break his neck or was his death due to a skull fracture. Jeff then talked easily about what the reporter who'd covered the accident said the autopsy had revealed. Fuss had a wound on the front of his head, left side, that had produced a fracture and a subdural hematoma that caused his death. The wound was caused by a hard object which would have been about an inch wide. The edge of the table in the boat's cabin was the certain culprit the police had concluded."

"There's something wrong with that picture," I objected immediately. "I was down inside the boat yesterday and I can tell you the table is not that close to the ladder, plus it is on the left side of the boat. Fuss always went down that ladder facing it and holding onto the railing facing the stern. If he fell backward, he would have hit the right side of the back of his head. The position of the wound is all wrong."

N.C. jumped in. "Al and I have a candidate for the weapon that would have caused that wound – the wrench we found on the apron of the sink in Fuss's utility room."

"I remember your mentioning that and the thin coat of rust as if it had been washed and left to air-dry," Coop said.

"Something Fuss would never do," added N.C. "He cared for his tools like pets. If he had washed it, he would have wiped it dry."

"OK. Let's say he was killed there at home and taken to the marina afterward in his own Jeep. How would the killer have gotten home? Was there an accomplice who had driven another car?"

Just then Sam arrived carrying a manila folder.

Now that Sam was present, Jill, who had been refilling coffee cups, asked, "The usual, Gentlemen?" and after receiving affirming nods and sounds, began preparing breakfast.

Sam opened the folder. "I've got a live suspect," he said rubbing his hands together. The guy's from Cedar, Homer Floyd. I was able to trace his exchanges with Fuss back four years. Twenty-one in all, if you can believe it. Good ole Homer would make some off-the-wall right- wing claim and Fuss would counter with a teasing jibe pointing up Homer's ignorance of the subject and usually follow that with a humorous suggestion."

"You mean a suggestion like, 'Stick that up --" said N.C.

"No, no, no. More like . . . I'll read one."

To the Editor:
Radical, leftist elitists like Mr. Quarrals have no place in this beautiful God-given country of ours. Certainly, no place in Leelanau County. You think you can

*muscle in and foist your sick views on people who have always lived their lives like their creator intended. You and your kind are contaminating rubbish.*

*Homer Floyd*
*Cedar*


"Here's Fuss's answer in the next edition of the paper."


*To the Editor:*
*"In answer to Mr. Floyd's letter in the November 18th issue. When disposing of your rubbish, Mr. Floyd, do you recycle? I'll bet not."*
*Frank Quarrals*
*Lake Leelanau*


"Yes," said Coop, "I can hear Fuss's voice there, but this is surely not the stuff that provokes murder."

"It gets better." Sam took another letter from the plle.


*To the Editor:*
*"It is clear to anyone with open eyes that liberals like Mr. Quarrals are only surface agents for a vast underground network whose aims conform with those we are told of in the Book of Revelations to be those of Satan. They intend nothing but the destruction of a God-fearing America. Our work is to be forever vigilant. We can't let vile weeds take root in our community! Pull them out!"*
*Homer Floyd*
*Cedar*

"Wow, that's a mouthful," I said.

"I think that's a threat, don't you?" Sam urged.

Coop said, "What was Fuss's comeback?"

*"To the Editor:*

*I read Mr. Floyd's letter to the Editor in the last issue of the Enterprise about 'underground networks' with interest. When I was a kid, my family was going on a trip to Mammoth Cave in Kentucky, but I got chicken pox and couldn't make the trip, so I'm excited about a chance to see the 'vast underground network' Mr. Floyd speaks of. Homer, if you know where the entrance is, please tell me."*

*Frank Quarrals*
*Lake Leelanau*

"I've got two reactions to these letters," said Coop. "One is I'm amused, but the other is critical of Fuss for engaging in this childish stuff."

I agreed. "I second that, but I also have a third concern. I've heard of cases over the years of a person who was on the edge of insanity being tipped over that edge by something like being taunted. Fuss's teasing might tip the balance for someone like Homer Floyd."

Sam added, "The woman who cleans our house twice a week, Martha . . ah, I forget her last name," Anyway, she comes from Cedar, so I asked her if she knew Homer. She laughed and said everyone in the township knows of Homer – few would admit knowing him. Seems he's a pain in the ass at Solon Township meetings. He loudly opposes anything that represents positive action. If a proposal can't be related to a Bible passage or to colonial America, he opposes it. He

106

works himself into such a lather that the meeting must pause while some 'friend' – neighbor or minister - can convince him he's done as much 'good work' as can be expected for the evening and he should go home and rest."

"What a nuisance," said Coop. "You'd think they'd bar him from the meetings."

"You'd think," agreed Sam, "Except a lot of people in his district agree with him. Anyway, out of curiosity, I looked up Homer's address and drove by yesterday. It's just outside Cedar. Kind of a rundown house with a fair size garden lot next to it. A hand-painted sign said 'Rhubarb – T.C. market Thur. Empire Fri.' We could run down to Empire and check out ole Homer tomorrow?"

The suggestion was not met with enthusiasm, but Coop, wanting to support Sam's effort said, "We need to check out Homer's alibi, at least."

"Are there other letter writers you'd rank as suspects, Sam?" asked N.C.

"There's a woman who is clearly unhinged, but unless she had help or is an amazon, she'd have a rough time with the physical part of the scenario we've been imagining. I'll check her out further."

"Vince, however, is our most likely candidate," I said. "He has a motive. He lied about going to Grand Rapids to close a real estate deal. He could easily have driven back from there after registering at the motel and killed Fuss that night."

N.C. who had been assigned to Vince shrugged. "Any suggestions?"

Sam offered, "The guys who worked with him at the realty office are not admirers of his. A conversation with one or more of them might give us a new lead.

Also, he was fired from his previous job – same thing there."

N.C. said, "I've got an appointment with one of those guys from the realty office right after I leave here."

"Good," Coop said, then added in the tone of having just remembered a detail. "Almost forgot. The time of death determined at autopsy was twenty-four to thirty-six hours before the body was discovered. That's a broad period; it covers Payne's fishing trip theory on the morning of the fourth, but it also includes the night of the third. So, scientifically, we're in the ball game."

"As if that meant anything to Payne," I grumped.

I noticed Sam with empty cup in hand trying to get Jill's attention.

"I've become aware that Jill hasn't been as attentive to our needs as usual. I wonder if it's because a young carpenter from Bigg's Construction has been coming in for coffee before reporting for work."

The others looked in the direction I indicated with a nod and saw Jill smiling down at a young man sitting at a table alone.

"I'll be damned," mumbled N.C. "Wouldn't you think there was one more cup in the coffee maker at his house? Why would a guy have to stop here for an extra cup do you suppose?'

"If my judgment of body language is unimpaired, I'll bet his breakfast and first cup this morning was made by his mother. Good luck to him," I said.

"And bad luck for us," added Sam.

"Yeah, but only for a few minutes. When the foreman's hammer comes down on the first nail of the day, this young buck's hammer had better come down one second later," N.C. said smiling.

And as predicted, a few minutes later Jill was there with the coffee carafe and a big smile that was more than our group of old codgers warranted. "The sun that warms one man can warm many." Confucius must have said something like that.

Coop got up from his stool saying, "The funeral is day after tomorrow. In movies, detectives always attend funerals in the hope that they'll learn something. Maybe we'll get lucky."

"After breakfast tomorrow, I'm driving down to Empire to the farmers' market. I'd welcome some company," said Sam in a voice that begged.

I said I'd be happy to tag along. N.C. and Coop then got on board as well.

"Anyone need anything from Menard's in T.C.?" I asked. "I'm going down there this morning. They've got a sale on a small propane barbecue I want to get."

The other three paused and gave that question a moment of thought before deciding they couldn't think of anything.

"If you're not in a hurry to spend your dough at Menard's," N.C. said to me as he got Itch up on his feet, "how about coming with me to talk to Joe McCord at the realty office."

"Sounds good. How'd you make the contact?"

"McCord and I played in a golf league one year at the Matheson Greens Golf Course."

"I was never there, but I've heard it said so many times that closing the course was a crime against humanity."

"Yes, a disaster of mythic proportions, like the expulsion from the Garden of Eden."

"Does this mean I've got to stand and listen to a lot of golf reminiscing before we get around to the subject of Vince DeSalle?"

"Probably."

We walked to N.C.'s place, where I left my bike and we took his car to Suttons Bay.

The realty office was just awakening when we walked in. The secretary, who greeted us had to clear her throat three times before she got her business voice adjusted. An agent standing at a nearby desk blinked an awareness that "the public" had just entered and a new workday had begun. Joe McCord had a small separate office space. Hearing the secretary speak to us he stuck his head out the door.

"Morning gentlemen, c'mon back here."

I realized I'd seen Joe numerous times at events like street art fairs. His outstanding feature was his height, at least six-six. You knew he played basketball in high school whether he wanted to or not. As I'd predicted, golf had to be remembered. Joe was saying, "After Matheson closed, I moved down to the Bahle course, where I still make the occasional attempt to hit the ball."

N.C. contributed, "I played at Veronica Valley until that closed too. I took that as a sign and gave my clubs to Goodwill."

My mind wandered to the question of whether the longer clubs Joe must use were more expensive than normal ones. Finally, the time came when N.C. turned the topic to Joe's take on Vince. I'll summarize. Little was known of Vince's early life. That is, it was not known which version of his early years was to be believed. An early, hard fact was that he was dishonorably discharged from the army. He had volunteered after high school and was given the heave-ho in less than a year. Reason unknown. This information had come from a former employer of Vince's whom Joe's boss had contacted after problems began to arise here. The boss had hired Vince on Fuss's recommendation without further vetting. It had to be admitted that Vince did present well. He was good looking from the viewpoint of all genders. He projected an earnest quality that encouraged trust. Stop right there! Because that's all you get. It was a big mistake to expect more. From Joe's point of view, the major problem was Vince's dishonesty—lies intended to cast himself favorably vis-a-vis the other agents, misrepresenting facts to buyers and making unfounded promises to sellers in order to receive bookings. Not high crimes, but actions that showed he had little respect for others and a poor comprehension of the consequences of his behavior. As Joe talked, a question grew in my mind; how could Carla love him the way she seemed to?

We walked back to N.C.'s car, got in and sat for a moment thinking over what we'd just heard.

"A rat for sure, but . . ." N.C. began and paused.

"But not a violent one," I furnished. "More the cowardly type, who would always be ready to scamper back to the rat hole . . . while spinning a reason for retreating that he thought made him look good. Makes me think of a certain politician."

"Well put, Al. Almost poetic."

"Thank you."

N.C. started the car and pulled away from the curb, throwing in, "He still has the best motive."

Joe had also told us he'd heard Vince had let it be

known that Fuss's house was for sale.

"Yeah, but there's something that nags. I mean, he knew he and Carla would be getting the house and Fuss's money when he died. What's the hurry? I mean, I've seen enough detective dramas and read enough mysteries to know that one takes a big step (and a self-destructive one if you're caught) to kill a rich relative when you're about to be cut out of the will. That wasn't about to happen here."

"Yeah, I know what you mean. Why would he need the money so suddenly?"

"Maybe gambling debts," I offered. "We need to find out if he spent time at the casino."

N.C. said nothing for a few moments. "I know a guy who goes there a lot. I'll ask him if he sees Vince there." N.C. was referring to the Indian casino in Pewshawbestown.

We parted at N.C.'s house with the usual promise to be, "in touch." I started on my bike ride home not knowing that I'd have more to add to the topic of Vince's motive for murder before the day was out.

As usual, Kato was standing waiting for me as I rode my bike up the drive. This time the body of a vole he'd caught was beside him. I have never known exactly what these "gifts" represent. The presentation is clearly related to me, but were they presents, or a proof that he was doing his part to rid the property of undesirable vermin? Or was he merely showing off his hunting chops? Personally, I had nothing against these little creatures, but I acted as if I had much appreciation for his effort.

"Way to go!"

# 11

I did some routine morning tasks including throwing a load in the washing machine and giving Kato clean water and some dry food to munch on, then, set out for Menard's. The giant store was located several miles south of my usual shopping grounds hence it was only something special, like the low price advertised for the barbecue, that brought me there.

Once I had the grill in my cart, I roamed the aisles replenishing things like glue (always hard in the tube or bottle when I needed some) and checked out. Maybe it was the topic of hamburger grills that brought a nearby restaurant/bar to mind. It and its mate on the north side of the city had a reputation for terrific burgers. It was well past lunch time.

After entering, instead of going directly to the dining area, I made a needed stop at the john, which was located at the rear near the curving bar. If I had not made that detour, the next phase of our investigation wouldn't have unfolded as it did, because when I re-entered the dining area to find a seat, my eye picked up a familiar shape – the back of Vince DeSalle's head. He was sitting in a booth half-way along the left side of the room. Sitting across from him was a woman who wasn't Carla. I stopped, retreated deeper into the bar area and took a seat on one of the stools. I couldn't see Vince's face, but the woman was facing me. She was younger than Carla. She was very attractive. Her manner of relating to him was not that associated with business or casual chats. Is "starry-eyed" a description still used? If it is, she was. Vince was putting on an award-winning performance for his friend - what an interesting and witty guy! And he was enjoying himself too, gesturing and laughing.

The bartender probably wondered why I had chosen to sit back in the dark end of the bar. Maybe I was a sad person wanting to drink alone. I ordered a draught beer and the burger I'd been looking forward to. The bartender put in the order with the kitchen and then served my beer. It came to me, then, that Vince might have to make the same trip to the john as I, and if so, he'd pass right by me. I called the bartender back and told him to make the burger to go. I continued to watch and became convinced that I was witnessing a love affair.

When my burger arrived, I asked for my tab and a paper cup. I left enough cash to cover the tab plus a generous tip, poured my remaining beer into the paper cup and quietly made my way out the door to my car. I didn't know which car in the half-full lot belonged to

Vince, so to be sure not to miss them, when they left the restaurant, I re-parked my car, backing into a space at the far end of the lot which would have a clear view of the door as the pair emerged from the building. My plan was to follow the girl's car. Parked next to me, and also backed into a space, was a bright, red Toyoto Yaris. I started on the hamburger that was good enough to take my attention away from my duties as a sleuth. In fact, as I ate and drank the beer my thoughts drifted to the question of the ethics of spying on another person's private life. Sure, Vince was a suspect in the murder of my friend, but was his extramarital affair any of our business? Did a legitimate question of motive, means and opportunity give license to raw snooping?

I was down to my last sip of beer when Vince and the woman came out. My abstract concerns with propriety vanished and I once again became an avid eavesdropper. She was indeed a very attractive woman when viewed in full. Go ahead, imagine your own vision of wholesome yet sexy, tallish yet agile, reddish yet blond, brainy yet personable, along with your idea of a perfect figure and that's what I was seeing. I snapped out of my thoughts about her when I realized they were walking right toward my car. Vince had his arm around her waist, and they only had eyes for each other. But, if they continued along their path, in ten seconds they'd be climbing my car's hood. If Vince were to look up and through my windshield now, he'd recognize me. Reflex-ively, I slid down in my seat. Later, I thought, so what? I had a perfect right to be sitting in my car in a ham-burger joint's parking lot. But at that moment, I felt like a spy about to be discovered by the Gestapo. I slipped down further. Now, if Vince were to glance into my car he would catch me in a totally asinine position, lying on my back looking up at him. I could just feebly wave and mouth, "Hi."

I heard the door on the driver's side of the Yaris parked next to me open. I couldn't make out what they were saying, but the girl's laughter was interrupted by moments of silence, which I filled in with kisses in my imagination. The car door slammed. I could hear Vince, but I could no longer make out her voice, since the window was closed on the passenger side of her car. That meant they were talking through her open window. It also meant he was not riding with her, or he would already have gotten into the car. Whew! I had escaped looking like a fool. The Toyota started up. I heard Vince yell something like, "I'll call." I wriggled up a bit to survey the situation. The Toyota had just moved out of the parking space and was heading for the exit. Vince was walking away in the other direction. I quickly started my car. I wanted to follow her—find out who she was.

She drove up to the lot entrance on Highway 31 and waited for a break in traffic. I became anxious now that Vince would drive up behind me and recognize me. It occurred to me that he might be going to the same place as his girlfriend, and I would be part of a moving sandwich. My old straw hat was on the seat beside me. I quickly put it on and tipped it to cover the back of my head. In reality, Vince probably has paid so little attention to me in the past that I could step on his toes, and he wouldn't know who I was. I was prepared for her to turn right - north. Everybody I knew lived north of this restaurant. My whole world was to the right of here. She moved, but it was a left turn she was making. I could have gotten killed along with the innocents I'd take with me, because without pausing or looking, I followed her.

I glanced in my mirror and saw Vince come to the driveway exit driving a pickup and turn north. But, where the hell was she going? She could be going shopping at Menard's just as I had. No. She drove past Menard's entrance. The only commercial buildings I'd noticed on this stretch of highway were a fence company and an "adult" video store. After several miles she hit her left turn-signal at a sign indicating five miles to Kingsley. Did she live in Kingsley? No. She drove through the blinker at main street and continued driving east. I should really give this up, I thought, and then I amended that to, "Just a little farther." Which I did until she came to highway 131 and turned south toward Cadillac? Grand Rapids? I couldn't follow farther even if I'd wanted to, because my gas was low. I drove onto the shoulder and got a pen and a scrap of paper and wrote down her license number, turned around and headed home. It was then that the words Vince and Grand Rapids banged against each other in my brain. Son-of-a-bitch!

I emailed Kirby when I got home with the news of my discovery. I'd tell the others in the morning. We'd have to trace the license number I'd taken down - find out who she was, what she meant to Vince, examine its relevance to Fuss's death.

This evening was to be a happy break from thoughts about the murder. Tonight, the innocent subject was art, the art of film. A meeting had been scheduled to begin preparations for next year's subscription film series at the Bay Theatre in Suttons Bay. My friends Betty and Tim Camden, who had been my hosts at the parade, Carole Stuart, with whom Beth Parker had stayed during her recent visit, and Marge Lawrence a friend from Traverse City and I were going to settle around a backyard table at the Camden's and begin to lay out the new season of "The Bay Goes to the Festival", the name we'd given our subscription film series (shortened by folks to "The Bay Festival.") The idea was to bring to the small-town theater current films that had won awards at international film festivals; films, residents would have little chance to otherwise see on a full theater screen. Our sixth season was coming up and we'd been very pleased with the community's response.

Our established routine early in the summer was to select the eight award winning films from the previous year's festivals to be shown for one weekend in each of the coming fall, winter and spring months. Brochures were then sent out in mid-summer that both described the films and served as a subscription application. We didn't have the manpower to handle phone calls, nor the setup for the internet – an old-fashioned snail-mail operation. At tonight's meeting we would begin to review and discuss last year's major film festivals.

As the others were momentarily occupied organizing their notes, Carole turned to me and said," Beth Parker told me about the sandwich lunch she shared with you in Fishtown. She enjoyed talking to you."

"She did? Yes, I enjoyed talking with her too. I can imagine she was a great roommate to have in college."

"She was for sure – all four years. We progressed through all the stages of late-night college wisdom together."

I liked that picture. It sounded like what a college

experience should be. Mine had been more chaotic.

"You were at an eastern college as I remember."

"That's right, Pennsylvania."

"Are you from Pennsylvania?"

"No, I'm from Connecticut and Beth was from Rhode Island."

"Why Penn?"

"Who can remember all the reason one did things in the past? We both had scholarships. That was a big factor, of course."

"My friend N.C. Dupree told me he remembered Beth making a 'MeToo' claim back when that movement was enjoying its peak attention. I expect she must have told you about that."

Carol hesitated, then nodded. "Yes of course. It happened just after her high school graduation – two boys about her age - never identified. No one she knew – they didn't go to her school."

"It was rape then?"

"Yes, where the one boy was concerned. The other held her down - thumbs in eye sockets. He didn't get his turn - thought someone was coming. "

"You say they weren't caught."

"No. The police did nothing. She had waited a day before reporting it and the police said it was too late to do a physical exam – which isn't true, but this was before DNA. Beth's parents were divorced. Her father lived in Arizona and her mother, while complaining to the police about their inaction, just wasn't a commanding enough personality to force them to act. It was this fact I believe which had the greatest impact on Beth – that her injury wasn't acknowledged by her community - she felt betrayed."

Wow, I thought. I suddenly saw a whole new dimension to unacknowledged injury that I had been blind to before. More to think about than this situation permitted now.

"How much of this did she relate in detail when she joined the MeToo revelations?"

"Only the fact of the rape and that the authorities largely dismissed her claim."

Marge had begun reading aloud a review of the Sundance Audience Award winner. I didn't ask Carole anymore about Beth Parker, but I could only half focus on the film festival work for the rest of the evening.

Walking out the door the next morning I was greeted with an immediate message: This is going to be one freaking hot day! The air was still and packed with potential heat and humidity, the sun hazy. I knew the back of my shirt would be wet before I pedaled halfway to the Bayo. When I arrived, I saw that Coop and N.C. were already there. I leaned my bike against the usual tree and took a moment to wipe the sweat from my face with the tail of my t-shirt. As I did, I heard Jill ask N.C. what those initials stood for.

"Stands for, 'No Comment'."

"Hey that's not fair," she pleaded, "We're friends."

N.C. looked down into his coffee for a long moment. "OK. You see it was like this, Jill. Back in the bayous where I was born, most of the young'uns were eaten by gators."

He paused, seeming to have given her a complete explanation.

"That's it?" said Coop. "You're saying that because alligators ate most of the kids, your mother named you

N.C.?"

"I think what he means," I put in, "is that since they were going to be eaten anyway, why take the time and trouble to come up with a whole name when a couple of initials would do."

N.C. nodded.

Jill stared at him in disbelief, mouth gaping. Certainly, he must be joking, and yet . . .

I changed the subject, leaving her in her quandary. I related in detail and with drama the story of my sighting of Vince and his girlfriend, and of my reckless pursuit of my quarry until I had to turn back because of a near empty gas tank. This immediately brought on a general discussion of the implications this held for our investigation.

Sam, who had arrived as I was telling my tale, made a summary statement. "So, he's been cheating with someone who might live in Grand Rapids. It could account for his trip to Grand Rapids to the motel, but it doesn't mean he couldn't also have doubled back here and killed Fuss, using the trip as an alibi. We need a name and address to go with her license plate number that you copied."

"For sure the police won't help us." I took the paper on which I'd written the number and laid it on the counter. Jill turned the paper so she could read it and then left.

"Did he cuddle in Grand Rapids and how long?" mused N.C.

"Not so fast." Sam raised his hand as if to halt the speculation. "This new discovery explains something that has puzzled us; why would Vince kill Fuss to get money, when it was a sure thing that Fuss was leaving everything to Carla—meaning Carla and Vince. Why the damned hurry? What about this; he wants to get a divorce and marry the new lady, but only after he gets his hands on his share of the inheritance? If he left Carla for his girlfriend before Fuss died, he'd only get half of what he and Carla own now. After Fuss's death, he shares in Fuss's estate as well. Bingo! Fuss dies before the divorce."

Sam had pronounced this with a tone of triumph. He'd solved the riddle of the Sphinx. We were all nodding in appreciation.

"What a bastard," mumbled N.C.

"That's true. What Sam just said gives Vince a strong motive to kill Fuss, but at the same time, if in fact he was with the woman that night in Grand Rapids, it also gives him an alibi." My saying this, I saw, had the same effect as saying, "You can eat all the ice cream you want to, of course, you will also gain two pounds."

"Ah," Sam countered. "You're making a flawed argument. Just because he has a girlfriend in Grand Rapids doesn't mean he spent that particular night with her. The girl doesn't have to know anything about the reservation at the motel, or that he was there only briefly that night."

Sam was right.

Jill having left the counter a few minutes before, returned now.

"Her name is Sharon Duval, Mission Oaks Drive, Grand Rapids," she announced with a satisfied smile. "A good friend of mine is the clerk at the Department of State Office in Suttons Bay. The office is closed now, but she was able to access the office computer from her home."

She was clearly happy to be a useful member of the detective team. There was something else in that smile, a teasing glimpse into the "sisterhood", a reservoir of shared information, that all my life I've suspected keeps the full extent of that special knowledge hidden from men.

"Good work," said Coop. "Now we need to learn how serious it is between Vince and Sharon Duval – a fling, or wedding plans."

What came to my mind was the sisterhood once again. I looked a question at Jill.

"My sister lives in Grand Rapids," she said. "I'll see if she can help."

Sam got up and announced, "Time we got started for the Empire farmers market and a good look at Homer Floyd."

N.C. slid off his stool and picked up Itch's water bowl and carried it around to the back of the building where it was kept.

Coop made a quick trip into the Bayo to the john. I walked my bike with N.C. and Itch to his house where Sam picked us up in his Audi Q8. I'm of the opinion that a ninety-thousand-dollar car is more for about vanity than utility. The excessive luxury can even erode one's moral character - the effect that wearing electrically heated underwear might have had on King Arthur's knights.

We were taking 204 to M22 and that south to Glen Arbor. The back seat, where N.C. and I sat was very soft yet firm, air-conditioning worked well - quiet, smooth ride. Perhaps my moral character wouldn't be compromised by a ride to Empire and back .

"Sam, please go around by way of the dunes," I

said as he was picking his way through the vacationers who wandered willy-nilly across the road in downtown Glen Arbor. "It's been years since I've been that way."

"Same here," said Coop.

So, instead of turning left at the supermarket, Sam continued straight ahead on M109. A few minutes later we were at the entrance to the Sleeping Bear Dune, and he drove into the parking area. At this early hour there were at least ten figures already struggling up the face of the famous dune, sliding backward half a step with each step upward. If you were going to attempt this challenge, early morning was the smart time to do it. We hadn't been smart those many years ago when Mary and I had toured this region. We'd figured a climb to the top was required of every spirited traveler, like riding in a gondola on a visit to Venice. It had been right after lunch on a sizzling August day. Half-way up I'd realized we'd made a mistake. The sane person, I mean the mature, sane person would think beforehand, "This is an ill-conceived idea. I don't need to prove I climbed to the top of a pile of sand. I don't need to look down at Lake Michigan from there. I've seen large bodies of water before, and I will not advance my understanding of the world by adding yet another viewing to my accumulation of 'viewings.'" But no, the idea dominating my sun-roasted brain had been that I must put one foot in front of another; anything else would be "quitting." Quitting what? Quitting nonsense? Well, as you must know, the sensation that trumps sane insight is the flood of self-congratulation you feel when you make it to the top, having made it in spite of your imbecility - made it without having to face loved ones in the hospital ER and say you're sorry, but you're now about to leave them. I exaggerate.

Half-way back down the dune that day, we'd met a woman climbing up who was a disturbing shade of purple and sweating profusely. She was younger than my wife and I, but badly out of condition. Most likely her only form of exercise had been walking to her car. One didn't need a medical degree to know her condition was dire. I'd stopped and spoken to her.

"Excuse me, but don't you think you'd better stop and rest?"

She'd looked at me as if my voice had come from the sky, as if what I'd said had no relevance in her reality.

"You look to me as if you need to sit down right here and rest – and then slowly go back down."

She'd turned her attention back to the sand that lay upward ahead of her and took another step – and another.

So, this moment was added to others for which I blame myself for being passive when a bold action was called for. Moments when I allowed an injustice or harm to prevail, because I didn't take command. After all, I could have thrown her down and waved my arms and yelled for a park ranger. (There were no cell phones back then.) Instead, I hurried to catch up to my wife, who had not witnessed this encounter, and I put the incident out of my mind. Well, I think you can see that I never accomplished that. I wondered even now, as I have before, what became of the woman. I hope she survived, and the experience convinced her to get in shape and stick with croquet.

About a dozen miles farther after rejoining M22, Sam turned right onto Main Street in Empire. Like other small villages on the peninsula, its permanent population (1188 in the last census) swells several sizes with the arrival of the summer crowd. Eight times out of ten during the winter months you could drive the three blocks of Main Street without seeing a soul. Not so now. People were carrying things, watering things, or talking to others all along the way with a concentration of folks at the end of the last block in front of the post office. Next to it on a narrow vacant lot the farmers market was located. Sam drove slowly past looking for a place to park. I had never been to this market and was surprised to see there weren't more than half a dozen stands. Our search for Homer Floyd wouldn't be a lengthy one. Hopefully, Mrs. Floyd had brought both her rhubarb and her husband today. Around the corner from Main Street and next to the post office, Sam found a spot to park. We four got out, Sam locked his car and we walked back to the market entrance. The early bird who had the first stand sold soap, handmade from hand-picked flowers from his garden. I was reminded that I missed the subtle scents of some of the soaps Mary used to buy. I never thought of buying anything like that for myself. Now, I sniffed several of the choices before buying a lavender scented bar and hurried to catch up with the other guys. They stood in front of a stand that sold "mini greens," basil and such with leaves the size of my hearing aid batteries. That's where they stood, but their eyes were on the next booth, where a table was loaded with rhubarb stalks. The woman tending it was busy with a customer. Our attention, however, focused on the man sitting behind her, his eyes fixed on the screen of a laptop. We four looked at each other with the same surprise and acknowledged conclusion, because the man was sitting in a motorized wheelchair. We turned and walked back to Sam's car, waited for him to unlock the doors and climbed in.

"So much for my best letter-writing suspect," Sam said, pulling away.

There was no way Homer Floyd had the physical requirements of our killer – without an accomplice, that is, and getting someone to help you kill somebody, because you were angry about the letters the intended victim had written to a newspaper editor just wouldn't happen in the real world. Nevertheless, it had been a pleasant outing.

# 12

I don't know who met for breakfast at Caballo Bayo the next morning, because I had an early appointment with Deb, my dental hygienist. Happily, all the teeth were still mine. They'd have to be re-capped, of course, if I were suddenly tapped to be a TV talk show host. I picked up some wine I'd ordered from Becky at Hansen's and then went home to change for Fuss's funeral.

The funeral service was held at Carla's church in Northport, where Fuss had only occasionally joined her. Entering the parking lot, I saw that the service was well attended. Fuss had many friends and acquaintances he'd made during the twenty years he'd lived here and, of course, many of those here would be Carla's friends.

After parking I gave a quick glance around the

lot: mostly the ubiquitous, look-alike SUVs and large pick-up trucks. Standing out like a sprinter among weightlifters, was an open convertible, a Porsche.

N.C. and Ruth were sitting on the right side of the sanctuary about halfway back from the alter. He saw me and waved, pointing to the seat he'd saved.

"Hell'uva turnout," he whispered. "I was thinking my funeral would just about fill out the first row."

"If we did it together, I'll bet we could manage to fill the whole row."

"I'm for skipping formal funerals and opting for having my ashes spread in the big lake from a boat."

"I get seasick."

He ignored me. "I got here early and had a conversation with Malcolm Gardner, he's the real estate broker at whose agency Vince worked. He said Vince is moving right along with putting Fuss's house on the market and plans to sell it himself as soon as the deed is transferred to Carla. Malcolm also heard that Vince has engaged an estate sale company from Traverse City. My Jewish friends have a word for it."

"Chutzpah," I supplied.

Sam came in with Coop and Joan. They found seats on the other side of the room. I couldn't see Kirby, but it was difficult to check the rows behind me.

The low buzz of conversation trailed off when the minister climbed the low dais before the altar to begin the eulogy. He was young, not more than mid-thirties, had a ponytail and a tattoo peeking just above his collar. Would central casting send him to Northport? Today? I mentally shrugged. Although, I knew Fuss's connection with the church was slight, the minister, now, proceeded to present a seamless and affectionate portrait of the man I'd known. The implication that he'd known Fuss well was unmistakable and dishonest, but I forgave him his lie. I was glad for it. I knew Carla and her kids were pleased as well, which was all that mattered.

Several times during his remarks the minister had made a hand gesture and looked away briefly towards his left. I began wondering if he had a mannerism or even a tic, until he finished and stepped down and I saw that it had been the urn containing Fuss's ashes he'd gestured toward. I hadn't known he'd been cremated.

Before he left the dais, the minister introduced a tall, thin man wearing a black linen jacket and soft collared shirt with no tie, whom he identified as Ben Randolph. If he'd had a clerical collar, I could have seen him as the church's minister easier than the man who gave the eulogy. He explained he had been the president of the insurance company that Fuss had worked for all his working years. He had flown in from Asheville where he had a summer home. He was a relaxed, experienced public speaker. He shared his memories of small, telling and endearing details of his friendship with Fuss. It made me envious not to have been there myself in those early years. He spoke of Fuss's active involvement in various local community projects in Jacksonville, the home office of the company. And of Fuss's odd little projects like maintaining a dispenser of cold, bottled water at the city's shuffleboard courts - "old people should not become dehydrated," Randolph recalled Fuss saying.

Randolph paused while we had our laugh, then he went on in a serious tone. "Fuss had this curious, and admirable, yet never satisfactorily explained – to me at least – involvement with the court. He had a contact in the police department who informed him whenever a young woman couldn't afford legal representation. Fuss would decide to sponsor certain cases and foot an attorney's fee himself. His reason for doing this, if asked, was, 'Everyone should have competent legal representation before the court.'"

It was an odd experience hearing things about a friend you thought you knew well that didn't jibe with the certain picture you'd formed of him. These weren't negative revelations - far from it – not like those you might read about of a person keeping a second family in St. Louis. This information once again pointed to the general truth that one never completely knows another person. What would my truth-teller say about me? What would I say if I told the whole truth . . . if I let myself know the whole truth?   Funerals can get you thinking deep thoughts.

Carla spoke after Randolph. What she said was heartfelt and touching her voice catching several times. I wiped away my own tears. She didn't speak for long, and I expected Vince to follow her, but he didn't. Just as well. His insincerity would have spoiled everything.

The minister again came forward and ended the ceremony with a prayer and a moment of silent remembrance and then thanked all for attending. Carla and Vince and their two daughters went to the front of the room to stand beside the minister while the rest of us began leaving.

Outside, the entire membership of the "Superannuated Sleuths" assembled at one side of the parking lot.

"Nice service," observed Coop. Probably the most

common phrase spoken after every funeral.

I then said what was foremost on all our minds. "What about the things this Randolph guy had to say – about Fuss's charity works?"

"Yeah," said N.C. "How did Fuss get involved with the court? I can see providing water for the shuffleboard court, but 'Everybody deserves to have legal representation before the court.' Where did that come from?"

In her usual decisive manner, Kirby put in, "The main question for us; does this help us with our investigation?"

"No way," said Sam. "That's all long ago and far away stuff."

"I expect you're right," she conceded, "Still I'm curious."

"So am I," I agreed. To myself, I thought I might try to contact Randolph.

No one else had anything to add. Everyone sensed, at the same time, that the conversation was exhausted. This is a critical moment in social relations; when all come to recognize the instant when it's time to say, "Nice having seen you. Hope to see you again soon." Or else, what had been a mutually pleasant exchange, now risks becoming awkward. For our group, the extra meaning lurking there was the realization that our investigation might have come to an end. Kirby, like a good leader, sensed this and moved seamlessly to reactivate her team.

"We must meet soon," she declared. "Tomorrow night – to go over all we've learned and decide on the most promising next step. Joan, can you host the team at your house tomorrow night,"

"Sure. Seven o'clock?"

Kirby looked at each of us for agreement. "Seven it is."

Heading to my car, I noticed a tall guy taking off his dark, dress suit jacket and laying it on the passenger seat of the Porsche.

At home I went about the daily repetition of household tasks. The meaning of the funeral still hovering in my mind gave a poignancy to these simple actions; like, how lucky I was to be able to be watering my geranium. How wonderful to sit down to sardines on toast for dinner.

I poured myself another glass of iced tea and went out and sat on my back deck. The mallards weren't on the pond. My thoughts returned to the funeral and particularly to the surprising picture of Fuss that had been furnished by his former boss. Like Kirby had said, it made one curious. Paying the legal fees for young women? That was strange. How does one suddenly decide to do a thing like that? Earlier, I'd thought about contacting Ben Randolph. I could call him saying I wanted to thank him for his warm remarks remembering Fuss – that was true, I did appreciate his remarks. I thought his effort to come all the way up here from North Carolina to honor his friend to be commendable. He needed to be complimented.

In my old age, I've come to recognize how many times I've passed up an opportunity to compliment another person, figuring my appreciation wouldn't be meaningful to them. On those occasions when I did, I saw how wrong I'd been.

I remembered a time when a well-known actress came to Detroit playing the lead in a play at the Fisher

Theater. Having liked the play, a friend suggested to my wife and me that we invite her to dinner. What a crazy idea! In a mood of "Do we dare?" we were able to contact the actress at the theater and our invitation was accepted. She was genuinely thankful for escaping another night alone in a hotel room. We had a great evening together and remained in contact afterward. Perhaps it took growing old before I cared less if the other person valued my compliment.

However, I was very comfortable sitting here sipping my iced tea and gazing out at my pond. Why take the trouble to call Randolph? I'd only be satisfying my curiosity. As Sam said, whatever I learned from him wouldn't likely help our investigation. I refocused my attention on the bucolic scene of pond and fields, but before long, I became aware I was again thinking of Fuss's curious behavior with the law courts. What the hell! I got up, went inside and dialed Carla's number.

Vince answered. I said I was sorry to disturb them this evening, but I had been touched by the words of Fuss's former boss and I wanted to call him and thank him for his remarks. I said I was hoping Carla had his telephone number.

There was a moment of hesitation, during which I was sure he considered brushing me off, but he said, "Randolph is here with us. He's spending the night and catching a plane in the morning. Just a minute."

I heard an exchange between Vince and Randolph. Vince was directing him to another phone to take my call.

"Hi, this is Ben Randolph."

"Mr. Randolph my name is Al Burke. I was a good friend of Frank Quarrals. I was just with a group of his other friends and the topic was your remarks today at the funeral. You gave us all a broader knowledge of Fuss than we'd ever had. I want to thank you for helping us know him better. The involvement he had with the court was especially eye-opening and if you have time, I wish you would tell me more about that."

It took a moment for Randolph to shift gears from talking to Carla and Vince to remembering his remarks at the funeral. "Yes, Mr. Burke, what were you interested in?"

"More details I guess you could say, like when did his interest begin? Was there a particular case? Anything to help me – and the rest of his friends understand."

"I think as I indicated before, I was not privy to the entirety of this subject. I had my questions also as you may imagine. There was, however, this special feature, which I did not bring out at the funeral. I didn't think this kind of detail would have been appropriate for that setting. You see, the cases all concerned young women who were openly accusing a man of sexual assault. I learned of this accidentally. I was very curious, so one day when Fuss was in my office, I asked him straight out to explain. He'd have preferred to keep mum on the subject, but I was a friend he couldn't put off.

"What he told me was this. If a young woman is assaulted, be it rape or less and she dares to file a complaint with the police, the police investigate. What they find decides what they do next. There may be positive physical evidence, but it may come down to her word against the guy's. He may flatly deny the charge, or may say the woman was a flirt and got angry when she was turned down. It may end right there, or the police may decide to refer the case to the prosecutor's office where it may go forward or not. Through all of this, the woman is pretty much on her own. Some progressive police departments have a social worker for the woman's emotional support, but usually unless she can afford to hire her own lawyer, there is no one to advise her about the law. By contrast, when a criminal charge is brought against someone the state provides that person with a Public Defender. What Fuss was doing was providing a young woman who lacked money with her own attorney through the whole ordeal."

I was totally surprised by what Randolph had said. Not only was this unexpected information about my friend, but I realized I'd never put myself in the place of a young woman making a complaint—facing hostility and strange legal machinery on my own.

"And he did this several times as far as you know?" I asked.

"I was not privy to the details, and I only came to know about this by accident. Fuss played it pretty close to his chest, but I believe he'd done this for years."

"You said something at the funeral about Fuss having a contact in the police department."

"Yes, he and the chief of police were good friends and the chief supported Fuss's program."

My head was spinning with this revelation. "Was he successful? I mean what was the outcome in these cases?"

"Sorry Mr. Burke. I've told you all I know. I didn't want to snoop. Obviously, he didn't want this to be public knowledge and I respected that."

The well had run dry. "Thanks, Ben, for sharing

this with me. It's most interesting and what's more, I'm wondering if he might have continued with this activity after he'd retired and moved here."

"It wouldn't surprise me."

I hung up and just sat there. I wanted to get my arms around all I'd heard, but I was having trouble. I wandered into the kitchen and turned on the electric kettle. I became aware that Kato was rubbing against my leg, and I looked down at him.

"Right my friend. It's past your dinner time."

I opened the cupboard where I keep the cat food, and he went over and stood at the spot where he always eats just like a patient restaurant diner waiting to be served. I put down his bowl then continued to make myself a cup of tea.

Stalling. That's what I was doing. I felt daunted by the task of matching this information about Fuss's interest in young women making claims of sexual abuse with the quiet guy I'd known. I took my cup and headed for the armchair where I do most of my reading – and reminiscing. I stopped short. But wait! Ben Randolph didn't really have complete information. How much was contributed by Randolph's own imagination? And what about my fascination with this information? Was I finding a side-issue to turn to, since we were failing to make progress on the main issue – Fuss's murder? Another bit of senior behavior, like beginning one project only to be easily diverted from another – start down to the basement to get a nail to hang a picture in the dining room, see the new furnace filter I'd bought leaning against the furnace and go ahead and install it instead. Then I'd notice I'd left the light on in the closet I use as a wine cellar and while turning the light off, decide to take a bottle upstairs for dinner. Back upstairs I see the picture lying on the dining room table. What's that doing there?

Yeah, maybe this was all procrastination. I was tired of thinking about it. I went to bed.

# 13

Another sunny July day. Fine by me. I hadn't heard that the fruit growers were concerned about the lack of rainfall, so all was well. I went about my morning tasks: making the bed (not doing so was the first step toward degeneracy I'd been told), feeding Kato and remembering to start the dishwasher. These done, I rolled my bike out of the garage.

Cycling over familiar, lightly trafficked roads fosters rumination much as mowing a large lawn will do. As you'd expect my thoughts went to the telephone conversation with Ben Randolph last evening. I had come to that stretch of road that had almost no shoulder, when suddenly I was jerked out of my rumination by an urgent and visceral sense of danger. The sound of a car approaching from the rear was abnormally loud and NEAR! Reflexively, I turned the handlebar to the right –

away from the sound. Headfirst, I plunged off the road and down the hillside landing first squarely on my back and then rolling and tossing several more times.

I lay there stunned. There was dirt in my mouth. Could I move? Slightly. Clear sky above me. I took a consciously deep breath and let it out. Then a "me" emerged from my mental chaos with the declaration, "I'm alive!" I was basing this on my seeing that there was sky above me and it was populated with clouds, and I'd never heard that either heaven or hell had clouds. I tried to move and then decided to rest and try again later.

It was at this point that I heard, "Al," being shouted. I answered, but anyone standing farther away than three feet would never have heard.

And then the person was there kneeling beside me – a familiar face, my neighbor, Jeff Springer.

"Are you all right? What happened? Can you move?"

All good questions.

"Jeff," I managed.

He had taken out his phone. "I'm calling an ambulance."

The prospect of falling into the unyielding, rules-dominated hands of bureaucracy caused me to plead, "Wait . . . a moment. I think I'm OK. Shaken up."

I began to put together in my mind that I'd just had a hell'uva fall – but I was . . . OK. Nothing better demonstrates the infirmity of advancing age than a fall. Up until age five you fall and bounce up again—that is you bounce up once you've accepted the impartial nature of gravity, but first you need your parents' assurance that nothing is out to get you. Then come the ages of falling and rapidly scrambling up again (ten through eighteen or later if you're an athlete). Next comes climbing up. Following this, a fall takes on an increasing magnitude of menace. After eighty the body shatters upon falling. Not in terms of x-ray evidence perhaps, but in terms of the impact's effect upon maintaining the tenuous communications between the body's physiological systems. (All shook up, stuffing knocked out, unstrung).

Motivated to avoid unnecessarily becoming entrapped in the medical protocol that would ensue once I was in an ambulance, I wanted to demonstrate my wellness to Jeff. I struggled to sit up.

"I saw you falling," he said. "I was coming around that curve," he pointed to the sharp curve in the road that lay just ahead of the point where I launched into space. "I happened to look out my window to the left and there you were tumbling down this hill. What happened?"

"I'm not sure. I had a sudden fear a car was going to hit me, and I must have turned off the road."

"There was a car – no it was a truck – that passed me - coming toward me - right after I saw you falling."

Jeff looked up the hillside. "I see your bike – up there in the weeds. Can you stand up?"

He helped me and I stood. I bent this way and that and encountered no pain.

"If you can, let's climb up to my truck."

The bike was about ten yards below the road. I had tumbled and rolled another twenty. Jeff helped me to the road and then into his truck, which was parked across the road. He, then, retrieved and inspected my bike.

"Looks like there's no damage to the bike," he said. "You must have become separated from it before you hit the ground."

I listened to what he was saying, but I was still so affected by the fall that I couldn't pay close attention.

"Why do you think you were afraid of being hit by the truck?"

I made myself remember that moment. "The sound of the engine was loud – unnaturally loud. I just . . . ran away from it."

Jeff thought about what I'd said and then walked back across the road and inspected the very narrow shoulder carefully. Returning, he reported, "The truck's tires left no mark on that bit of shoulder." He paused a moment and then added, "Must have taken his eyes off the road for a second. Either that, or he tried to hit you. Either way, if you hadn't left the road and launched yourself down the hill, He probably would have hit you for sure!"

Now I was paying attention. "What kind of truck was it?"

"I hardly noticed. I was focused on you – falling, but my impression was of a big pick-up like an F-150— dark color. You're sure you're OK. Maybe we should go to urgent care and let them take a look."

"No, I only want to go back home and sit down for a while. I'll be fine."

When we got there, he walked me into the house and left saying he'd have Susi check on me later. I sat at the kitchen table for a while before it occurred to me that the guys would wonder about my not coming to breakfast. I took out my phone and called N.C.

He answered, "Morning Al, what's up?"

"Morning N.C. Me, that's what was up – up and then down. I had a little mishap with my bike. I'll tell you all about it at our meeting at Coop's place tonight."

"You fell? Are you OK?"

"Perfectly, but I'm skipping breakfast this morning."

"Anything I can do for you?"

"Nothing at all, but thanks."

I heard him explaining to others what had happened to me and then he was back on the line.

"Too bad you're not here to see Sam's new Hawaiian shirt. Jill had to put on her sunglasses."

"I know it breaks his sartorial rules to wear something two days in a row but ask if he'll make an exception and wear it again tomorrow."

"Just a minute – Coop is asking if you're sure you're OK."

"I'm all right and my neighbor's wife is coming by soon."

"Sounds good. I'll call you later."

At my age, one dreads the misstep that can convert a trouble-free life into a possibly permanently burdened one. I was reassuring myself that I had dodged the bullet once again, when the doorbell rang. That would be Susi Springer and I hesitated to answer the door. Would she come in and cancel my wish to make little of the fall – find something that would call for that ambulance yet?

She opened the door and called out, "Al, It's Susi."

"C'mon in. I'm in the kitchen."

Susi was one of those people that you just know had a happy childhood with parents and siblings she knew she could count on for reliable support. And today, this is what she offered everyone free of charge. What an asset she would be working in a doctor's office.

She came into the kitchen and stood looking at me for a long moment.

"Take a chance," I said, "have a seat."

She smiled. "Well, your smart-ass circuits are intact."

"Seriously, I think I'm not injured. I know that I won't be able to move tomorrow, but that doesn't count."

"Headache?"

I shook my head.

"Back pain?"

I moved around in my seat. "No."

"Have you urinated?"

"Ah, no."

"Do you think you could?"

"You're thinking blood?"

"I'm thinking no blood."

I got up, went to the toilet and back. "Looked normal."

"Good. I see you're walking in a straight line."

"Oh my God, I haven't done that for years."

She liked that. "You were on your way to breakfast at Caballo Bayo, right?"

"That's right."

"Which means you haven't had breakfast. What'll it be?"

"Toast with honey and coffee."

She stayed for about an hour chatting and drinking coffee. She mentioned seeing Kato prowling around their barn. "He reminds me of a cop on a beat making his rounds checking every door to see if it's open."

"He's really casing your joint."

"He's welcome to all the mice he can steal."

"Mice are sport, not food. He only eats the most expensive cat food – he checks the label."

While it was a pleasant talk we had, I felt she was really checking for signs and symptoms all the while. An hour seemed to satisfy her.

"Do you have any ibuprophen in the house?"

I nodded.

"Do you take blood thinners?"

"No."

"Then take six hundred milligrams," she said and left.

Half-an-hour later, N.C. yelled, "Anybody home?" as he and Sam walked in – Sam and his pulsating shirt.

With the two of them right here, I knew I had to describe what had happened beyond "I fell off my bike." So I included the truck, flipping down the hillside, and that my neighbor thought the truck was like a Ford F150.

They ran through a review of my body's systems and then N.C. said, "It really pisses me off that the guy didn't stop. He must have realized you fell. I've thought of this before when I've heard about a hit and run. In a second the driver can envisage the life they've built for themselves come tumbling down - liability, jail time if they'd been drinking, also there's the damage to their social image. Then comes the thought that if they just keep driving, they'll escape that disaster. What is not faced up to at that moment, and what costs more in the long run are the mental costs of leaving the scene – guilt in its many forms and the lingering fear that they'll be discovered."

I hadn't given any thought to the driver of the truck. Hearing N.C., now, I realized I'd always held the hit and run driver to be the lowest of the low. Driving away was as good as turning in your membership card to the community.

I'd had enough thinking about my fall. "Anything of note at the Bayo this morning?"

That brought blank looks on two faces. N.C. laughed and said, "Trish had a big problem attending to us when her mind was definitely on that young carpenter."

"We can only hope Biggs starts a new job at the far end of the county," Sam added.

At the door, as they were leaving, I mentioned that I'd talked to Ben Randolph last night.

"Ben Randolph?"

"Fuss's old boss," I said. "The guy who spoke at the funeral. He told me some interesting details. I'll tell you what he said at the meeting tonight."

N.C. started down the steps and then turned back. "You know who has a Ford F150? Vince DeSalle."

# 14

The Spences lived in a comfortable house over-looking the seventeenth fairway of the Leland Country Club. On summer days the golfers passed at regular in-tervals, pausing, swinging with varying skill, depositing a few stray balls on the Spence's lawn and then moving on. In the twilight that followed, a family of deer would graze on what must have seemed like a perfect pas-ture. Summer evenings here were peaceful. Usually. This night's meeting opened with N.C.'s rant.

"Vince almost killed Al! He tried to run him over. The sheriff's got to pick him up!" N.C. began loudly proclaiming this when Coop opened the door to him. We had driven separately, because N.C. had to leave the meeting early. He continued demanding Vince's ar-rest as we assembled in the Spence living room. Kirby managed to get us seated and suggested, in a calm, controlled voice, that I should describe my experience myself. I, then, tried to relate the event in the same neutral manner as hers with only mixed success. It's difficult to relive a flight through the air with the expectation of a disastrous landing, without some emotion seeping into the narrative.

Kirby, with Joan Spence reinforcing her calm logic, was able to extract the fact that Jeff Springer only thought the truck might have been an F-150, while pointing out that Ford had been successful in selling at least fifty trucks like it in Leelanau County. True, but I leaned toward N.C.'s version.

"Yeah, but Vince has a motive. He knows that Al has been nosing around. He found him at the boat with that deputy and he knew damn well what Al was doing there."

"It's a very disturbing possibility," admitted Kirby, "but for the moment, let's put it aside in order to review the whole of our investigation."

The problem with having a discussion of a hot topic with a rational person is that they get in the way of healthy rage. Would we have the exciting saga of the Viking raids if they'd had a level-headed leader who had counseled moderation? "After all guys, that swag is really not ours. It belongs to those other people."

Coop took advantage of the break following Kirby's reasoning to get our drink orders. Kirby reminded us that we were assembled in order to review the progress of our investigation and set out our immediate course.

Sam joined Kirby reluctantly. "Yeah, let's review what we have so far, but I'm with N.C., Vince is our man!"

Kirby reflected the attitude of the fourth-grade teacher who has just brought the class into order so that the arithmetic lesson could resume.

"When we adjourned several days ago, several assignments had been made," she continued. "Perhaps reports on those would be the best place to begin with tonight."

Coop paused his drink distribution. "I was to check on the autopsy. It went easier than I'd imagined. I met the *Enterprise* editor for coffee. He said right off that he knew Fuss and I had been friends and told me what his reporter had discovered about the autopsy. He said Fuss had died from a subdural hematoma caused by a depressed fracture of the skull following a blunt object blow about an inch wide. The wound was in the left frontal region."

I commented on Coop's report. "That wound fits with what N.C. and I found in Fuss's house – the wrench that was lying on the drain board of the sink in the utility room. And it conflicts with what the cops want to believe, that he hit his head on the table in the boat. Fuss always climbed down the companionway ladder facing the steps. If he'd fallen backwards on the table, the wound would be on the right side of the back of the skull."

Kirby made a note in a notebook, then read from the same book, "Sam, you had an idea that one of the people Fuss feuded with in the *Enterprise* could be a suspect. How about that?"

"Well, my favorite candidate was a bust. The guy turned out to be incapacitated—not capable of carrying Fuss to the boat. I haven't found another likely candidate in that quarter."

"You were also going to learn the terms of Fuss's will, Sam."

"It hasn't been probated, but I'd be very surprised if all didn't go to Carla. I'll keep on it."

Kirby studied her notebook a moment. Then looked toward N.C. "You were going to check Vince's alibi. Was he in Grand Rapids?"

"That's complicated," N.C. replied. "He went and registered at the motel there, but the night clerk didn't see him after he registered. Even if he stayed part of the night, he had time to drive back here, kill Fuss and return to Grand Rapids. But now Al has discovered that Vince has a girlfriend who lives in Grand Rapids. He might have gone there and stayed with her and booked the motel just to cover up his real reason for the trip."

This was the first Kirby had heard of the girlfriend. She hadn't read my email. "Well, well. A girlfriend. I wonder what this means as a motive for murder?"

"N.C. and I have speculated about that," I said, "If Vince is serious about this woman. Sharon Duvall is her name. If he's intending to leave Carla and marry her, then it would be to his great financial advantage to have Fuss die and Carla inherit his estate before he divorced her. If, on the other hand, he divorced Carla before Fuss died, his settlement with Carla wouldn't include Fuss's assets. So, he'd have a huge motive to kill Fuss now."

"Interesting," Kirby said, mulling over what she'd just learned.

Joan broke the silence as a summarizing observer. "After all has been said and done, it seems we have but one suspect—Vince DeSalle."

"Hell yes! He tried to kill Al today!" N.C. exclaimed.

"Hear Hear!" chimed in Sam. "This Payne guy, the stand-in sheriff, has got to believe us now."

I think we were all imagining Payne's reaction to our argument, when Coop said in a sober tone, "We have a problem, as was pointed out earlier, what proof is there that it was Vince driving the truck that ran Al off the road? And although Fuss's death, coming when it did, was to his financial advantage if he were planning to divorce Carla, that in no way is proof that Vince is the murderer. We found a wrench that could have been a murder weapon, but then again . . ."

Knowing he had just rained on our parade, Coop got busy passing appetizers.

"Any fresh ideas?" Kirby said, smiling mischievously.

There were no contributions. After a moment I said, "I have some new information. Not anything that will help, but interesting. I talked to Ben Randolph, Fuss's old boss, after the funeral. He was spending the night at Carla's and I spoke to him on the phone. I told him that I thought his coming and relating his early memories of Fuss must have been very helpful for Carla. I then said that his description of Fuss's involvement with the court had piqued my curiosity and wondered if he could say more about that and he did. It turns out Fuss was paying for legal representation for young women who had made formal charges against guys who had sexually assaulted them. Randolph explained that unless she could afford a lawyer herself, at no time in the whole process of making the complaint, possible charge and trial is the young woman furnished legal counsel. That's what Fuss was doing and doing for a long time as far as Randolph was aware, and he said he wouldn't be surprised if Fuss had continued doing this here."

"What a strange thing for Fuss to focus on. What would motivate him, unless Carla had had a bad experience—something like that." This was Joan, who verbalized what we were all pondering.

Sam asserted, "We'll never know that. Like Al says, it's interesting, but it doesn't help us with our problem."

N.C. spoke up. "There were those checks for large amounts that we saw in Fuss's check register. Could they be related to what Randolph talked about?"

I thought back to when N.C. and I looked through the check register. "Yeah, when we were searching Fuss's house looking for any kind of clue, we came across his check register. Most checks were for small amounts like electric bills and so on, but there was the occasional large check . . . several thousand . . . written to a B . . . B what, N.C.?"

N.C. concentrated, closing his eyes to envision the pages of the check register. "Campbell! B. Campbell," he announced, smiling, pleased with his feat.

"Is there an attorney around here named B Campbell?" I asked looking around the group.

"Ah, yes," Kirby answered with a smile. "Blake Campbell, or 'Cannibal' as other attorneys call him. He's famous in northern Michigan. It's said that no insurance company will go to trial against him, they just settle out of court. How much money were these checks for?"

N.C. and I looked at each other. "There was a big one, like ten thousand," I said.

"Right, and a couple around two thousand as I recall," N.C. added.

"Then Blake Campbell is not the man," Kirby said laughing. "His fees are the highest in the area. If you'd said thirty thousand, then maybe."

"Maybe he has a sliding scale for the elderly," I joked.

"Afraid not. He earns his nickname."

Joan getting up to pass a bowl of nuts around observed, "Still, the origin of this unique interest is intriguing. Does any one of us know Carla well enough to ask her?"

No one spoke up.

"Could stir up bad memories. Better left as is." This was Sam, and I could tell by his body language that he thought we were wasting time on a side issue.

"We do have," Kirby quickly put forward in a tone and cadence calculated to stimulate a positive spirit, "a very likely suspect to present to Sheriff Hoss Davis when he returns from vacation in a few days. We can forget about this Payne fellow; Sheriff Davis is our man. There are too many facts pointing to murder and to Vince DeSalle as the murderer to be dismissed. I have no doubt Sheriff Davis will take us seriously."

That summarized the extent and limit of our effort to find Fuss's murderer. Joan allying herself with Kirby's intent to end on a high note, picked up the rhythm by announcing dinner.

"The chef tonight is offering Costco's Italian sausage and beef lasagna. My contribution is salad. Sam brought two bottles of Barolo, which I'm told is not a bad wine for a non-Leelanau vineyard."

"I'm going to miss a great meal," said N.C. standing. "As I told you earlier, my sister had planned dinner tonight for her nephew and would like me to be there."

He said his good-byes and left.

I enjoyed my meal, but I found getting up from the armchair daunting, because of increasing stiffness and later, making my way to the car after saying goodnight to the others, required determined effort. At home, I dropped my clothes on a chair and didn't bother attempting to put on pajamas before falling into bed.

# 15

In the morning, I awoke to find I couldn't move. No, I wasn't paralyzed, but all my muscles had joined together in rebellion—a general strike. I couldn't just lie there and wait for things to improve. That might take all day – days. A hot bath was the answer. I hadn't trusted getting into and especially out of my bathtub for a year. It had been showers exclusively. A shower didn't seem to offer the relief I needed. A spa with steps down into a hot Jacuzzi tub assisted by a therapist was the ticket. Dream on. My shower has a railing and a seat. I sat with the water pouring over me until the hot water tank was exhausted. The improvement was enough to enable me to feed both Kato and me. Entertaining no thought of activity beyond sitting, I took a cup of coffee to my easy chair and began reviewing our meeting last night.

I guess the information about Fuss's legal support of young women had had a greater impact on me than it had on the others. It was thought to be interesting, but of no value to our main purpose. Maybe that's right, but I wasn't satisfied. Perhaps it was due to having talked to Ben Randolph and having heard the puzzlement in his voice. He'd wondered all along what lay behind Fuss's costly commitment. On an impulse, I turned on my iPad, clicked on Safari and typed in Blake Campbell, Traverse City. There it was: Blake Campbell attorney at law with an address on Midtown Dr. I didn't know that street. I checked the time on my pad. 9:40. I stared at the phone number for several seconds as if it could make up my mind for me. What did I have to lose? The "Cannibal's" receptionist could only tell me to get lost politely - or impolitely. I reached for the phone on the table by my armchair, and then hesitated. I could hear better on my cell phone, because it was linked to my hearing aids. It was in the pocket of my pants that I'd dropped last night on the chair by my bed. I made the slow, stiff walk there and back, then entered the number.

When she answered, I told the receptionist my name and that I wanted to make an appointment to see Mr. Campbell concerning a former client of his, Frank Quarrals, who had recently died.

"May I ask what it is you want to talk to Mr. Campbell about, Mr. Burke?"

I should have known that would be her response, but I hadn't worked out in my mind how I'd explain what I wanted to find out from her boss.

I said, "My friends and I think Frank Quarrals was murdered. I want to ask Mr. Campbell if he knows anything that would help us." It just came out.

There was silence for several beats before she said, "Just a moment."

Was she dialing the police on another line to report a crazy man talking of murder? Instead, a deep baritone voice said, "This is Blake Campbell. What exactly is on your mind Mr. Burke?"

I calmly laid out our suspicions about Fuss's death and our partial knowledge dealing with his legal "charity."

In a tone I'd call collegial, Campbell said, "I'd like to talk to you in my office, Mr. Burke. I'll be free at five o'clock; would that work for you?"

It took a nano-second to decide. It took longer to catch my breath to answer, "Yes. Yes, that's a good time."

I didn't know what to make of his response. I stopped wondering and called N.C. and told him about the call.

"You'll come with me, won't you?" I urged.

"If he'll give us a group rate. Do you think he charges by the minute?"

"He made the appointment with me, not the other way around. What's *our* fee schedule?"

"Last night you were walking like the tin man in the Wizard of Oz; I'll drive. Better make it four o'clock. There's traffic at that time."

I got up and returned to the bedroom to dress and make the bed. I discovered then that the phone call to Campbell had done wonders for my flexibility.

Blake Campbell's address was a two-story brick building on Midtown Drive, a street that ran along the Boardman River only a few blocks from Front Street.

The other buildings on the street looked like residential duplexes. We parked and walked to the entrance where a single bronze plaque read "Blake Campbell, Attorney at Law."

"Looks like the whole building is his," observed N.C.

Upon passing through the entrance we came to a solid glass door through which we could see into a waiting area with comfortable seating. The door had no handle, so I pushed against it and it didn't budge. I was looking for a doorbell, when a smiling face appeared on a screen above the door and a pleasant voice asked, "Can I help you?"

I looked up at the smiling face and spoke to it.

"I'm Al Burke and this is my friend, N.C. Dupree. Mr. Campbell is expecting us."

The glass door slid into the wall. We walked inside and were greeted by the same smiling face – a receptionist sitting at a desk to the right.

"You gentlemen may go right up to his office," she said indicating the elevator across the room from her desk.

As the elevator door closed, N.C. said, "That's a hell'uva security setup. I'd bet anything that was bullet-proof glass in that door."

"If your nickname is "Cannibal" maybe you'd need it."

We stepped out of the elevator into a large, well-lit room with large windows onto the street. The wall across from us featured the floor-to-ceiling shelves of law books one has come to associate with a law office. To our right was a conference table and to the left another desk and another smiling secretary, this one much older.

She said, "Hi," and would have followed it with more, but the door to Campbell's inner office opened and the man himself filled the doorway. He was the guy I'd seen at the funeral getting into the Porsche. He spoke in a relaxed deep voice with friendly overtones. I wasn't expecting this from a Blake "Cannibal," who knew he was about to be asked for intimate information about a client. It made me wary.

"Welcome gentleman. Please come in."

Come into my parlor said the spider to the fly.

N.C. and I followed his gesture and entered his office. It was large with a window overlooking the Board-man River. Instead of an expansive single pane, the window was broken into a dozen smaller panes, causing one's attention to return to the interior space. It was a working office - dark wood desk on which were stacked papers and files with a well-worn leather swivel chair behind it. I'm not sure about other decorating features; my mind was on the man. He was tall – six two or three - tanned and fit, dark hair shot through with gray and the quiet confidence of a man who knew what he was capable of and was satisfied with that much. He waved us toward a grouping of two armchairs and a couch in the corner of the room to the right.

As I sat down, I said immediately, "I'm Al Burke, who spoke to you on the phone, and this is my friend N.C. Dupree."

"I'm Blake Campbell, as you know. Please tell me about yourselves and how you came to call me."

His attitude was friendly - but reserved. I might as well say right here what I came to conclude after fur-ther dealings with him: his reputation as a formidable opponent in court was based on an instant surety that what he said could be taken straight to the bank. Juries must have arrived at the same impression. I proceeded to tell him about our little breakfast club and what we came to know of Fuss's personality and how the so-called facts upon which the sheriff was basing his opinion of accidental death didn't fit with our knowledge of our friend. I added our "evidence": Oscar in the utility room, position of the head wound and the phony lunch with forbidden pear.

"At his funeral, as you know, Fuss's – that was the nickname we all knew him by – Fuss's former boss spoke about his contributions to a lot of charities in his hometown, Jacksonville, but the activity that stood out for us was his legal support of young women who had charged some guy with sexual abuse. Now because we guys in our breakfast club didn't believe the accidental death bit, N.C. and I searched Fuss's house for any evidence that we were right – that he was murdered. During that search, we scanned his check register and discovered he had sent you several large checks . . . "

"And you wondered if they indicated a continuation of this same legal support you'd heard about at the funeral?"

"That's right." N.C. said, "And if so, it occurred to us that the accused guy in a rape case would have a motive to eliminate the person supporting his accuser."

Campbell leaned back in his chair and crossed his legs. "Reasonable thought, and you've wondered how much I'd be willing to say, because of client confidentiality."

I nodded.

"Frank was not a client. He and I were partners.

So, I'm free to talk about our relationship if I see a good reason to do so. He came to me . . . maybe ten years ago. He told me about the legal support he'd provided in Florida and said he wanted to continue that here. He explained how his interest began when he'd learned about a young woman who'd charged the son of a local big shot with rape. Immediately, the father was able to mount a campaign to cast the woman as a slut. A newspaper interview with the assistant prosecutor who'd been assigned the case revealed that the father's efforts had taken root. The young woman had no money to afford an attorney of her own. Frank had thought at the time that if she'd had legal counseling it would have given her accusation more credibility on the law enforcement and prosecution side of the equation and would also have bolstered her confidence through the ordeal of a trial. So, Frank hired the best lawyer in that part of the state. With him in the young woman's corner, the complexion of the proceedings changed. The chief prosecutor took over the case and the man was convicted.

"Frank then formed an alliance with the chief of police, a long-time friend of his, to alert him to any similar cases. I think he said he was involved in eight additional cases over the years. Not all resulted in convictions – not all were guilty. Of main importance to Frank was that the woman was not alone in court. He came to hire me as an attorney. However, I was impressed by what he told me and proposed a partnership; I would provide the legal counseling and he would cover the ancillary expenses like private investigators' fees. Investigative inquiries into the activities of the accused can be beyond the budget of a county prosecutor's office. We would try to supply that information. Frank agreed to my proposal. We've collaborated on six cases in Grand Traverse and Leelanau County. There have been many more cases of sexual abuse in the time we've been associated, of course, but the great majority of the women involved have been able to afford an attorney's fee."

Campbell interrupted his narrative. His expression suggested to me that a memory of Fuss had come to his mind.

He went on, "It was a good, frictionless partnership. I'll miss it. I'll continue our program, of course, but it won't be the same."

I shook my head in disbelief. "Jeez, how you think you know someone well and really have no idea . . ."

"I'd like a cup of coffee." Campbell said, "How about you?"

Yes, we were both in the mood for coffee and agreed. Campbell got up and opened the door and spoke to the secretary in the outer room.

Upon sitting again, he said, "What intrigued me when I spoke to you on the phone, Mr. Burke, was your theory that someone accused of rape would have a motive to kill a person giving support to his accuser. You see, I said Frank and I had worked together on six cases. That sixth case is ongoing right now."

This got our attention big time. The secretary returned and distributed the coffee while Campbell went on.

"There are things about this guy – the guy accused of rape – that make what you're suggesting possible . . . but on the other hand, I wonder. I want you to tell me everything you know or suspect about Frank's death. I'd like to record what you say, if that's OK with you."

Whoa, I thought. I suddenly felt out of my depth. Echoing in my mind were the things that happened when people had been recorded saying something that then had them before Senate investigating committees. I had been settling into a comfortable intimacy with this man, but now I reminded myself, N.C. and I had wandered into the inner chambers of the "Cannibal." N.C. decided the issue.

"For the present, let's just tell you what's been on our minds. If you agree that we're right, we can always write something out later."

With a knowing smile Campbell said, "Fair enough."

We proceeded to relate the course of our thinking about Fuss's death and all that we had discovered; one or the other taking up the tale in turns.

Campbell had been listening intently, elbows on the arms of his chair with his hands forming a steeple that he bounced against his lips. I ended with the repetition that we thought that possibly someone accused of rape would want to eliminate the person giving support to his accuser.

Immediately nodding, he said, "I understand your dissatisfaction with the Sheriff's Department's stance, and I empathize with your frustration at not discovering more conclusive evidence. As you said, you've come hoping you'll find it here. First, it's very unlikely that someone could know of Frank's partnership with me. His activity was limited to writing checks. Still, it's possible. So, I'll tell you about the most current case we were engaged with. It's a charge of rape against a guy named Lawton Preskorn. His father owns Preskorn

Industries, an aerospace contractor. The son is as close to the stereotype of the rich, spoiled brat as you'll come across. Since grade school he has freely acted out his attitude of, "I'll do whatever I feel like doing," sure that his father – who I'm sure gets vicarious pleasure – will be there to bail him out. In the present case, Lawton was claiming an alibi of being with a friend at the time of the rape. Investigation we undertook knocked that in the head, so now he's claiming the sex was consensual. That, of course, is a frequent defense of predators, especially those who have some celebrity or other marketable worth, hoping to sell the idea that any woman would desire them and try to bed them. Lawton Preskorn – or 'Law' to his friends – actually, he'd picked up the nickname, 'Lawless' in high school – would like to think he's irresistible to women. He's twenty-eight and has been getting a salary as a 'consultant' from his old man's company since he squeaked through an Ohio liberal arts college to which his father had made heavy contributions.

"He's been accused by women before of sexual assault. Not violent rape, but of aggressive, unwanted crossing of boundaries. If a third-party appears, Lawton quickly retreats making out he was joking. He's a first-class prick."

A thought came to Campbell. "Although it may be a coincidence, the assault he's being accused of took place on his boat, the boat he keeps at the Northport Marina. I wouldn't have thought Preskorn could have known about Frank. But his father did hire a private investigator, so I suppose it was possible. But murder is a reach. What had he to gain by killing Frank? It's a question I've got to think about, and I'll have our own

164

investigator check out Preskorn's alibi for the critical time, since you have convinced me that Frank was murdered."

As he ended that thought, his expression showed another idea had his attention now.

He said, "Frank claimed his interest in providing the legal support we've talked about began with the case in Florida. I've wondered if maybe it was more personal. I've wondered if it involved his own daughter. Perhaps if you had a conversation with her . . . you never know."

He stood up. "Pleasure meeting you, Mr. Burke - Mr. Dupree."

"Please call me, Al."

"And N.C."

"Fine and it's Blake here. I'll be in touch."

# 16

I knew that both Coop and Sam wouldn't be able to make breakfast at the Bayo the next morning, so I called a meeting of the team for that evening night at my house to talk about our meeting with Campbell. Here was a chance to try out my new barbecue grill. Amidst many interruptions that morning at the café, N.C. and I had done our best to tell Jill the story of Fuss's philanthropy. It happened that she knew of a friend of a friend in the county who'd experienced Blake Campbell's guidance through the ordeal of charging her employer with sexual assault.

"Well, I'll be damned," N.C. muttered. "Right under our noses."

That evening I arranged my lawn chairs and two kitchen chairs in a semicircle overlooking my pond. Beer, a bottle of pinot grigio and soft drinks were in a tub with the bag of ice I'd picked up at N.J.'s Market. The menu featured hamburgers on my new grill. The topic of conversation as we assembled was the fewer number of mosquitos this summer. Here we were sitting by a pond at sundown and not a critter in sight.

"Lack of rain," explained Coop. "If we'd had a few rainy days in a row, we'd be slapping away - or running inside."

"'Rain, rain stay away. Come back some other day,'" sang Kirby.

"I'll drink to that." Sam raised his glass of wine.

I began by describing my conversation with Ben Randolph and his enlargement on the story he'd told at the funeral, explaining that the young women Fuss was assisting had been charging a guy with sexual assault. N.C. and I proceeded then to relate the story Blake Campbell told us of being Fuss's partner in continuing to do right here in Grand Traverse and Leelanau Counties what he'd been doing in Florida. We finished with Campbell's revelation that the case he and Fuss were engaged with at the time of Fuss's death was a young guy accused of date rape aboard the boat he keeps at the Northport marina. N.C. ended the story with Campbell's description of Lawton Preskorn.

When we'd finished Kirby mused, "I was just thinking of times when I've heard a stunning fact that should have gotten my attention. but it didn't take hold in my brain. I'm talking about hearing Randolph describe at the funeral this significant involvement Fuss had in providing young women with legal counsel. I should have reacted with 'Whoa! What's this all about?' but I didn't. Maybe this obtuseness occurs whenever the fact is so big that it calls for more attention than I can give it at that moment, and I simply put it aside."

"I hear you," N.C. agreed.

"What Ben Randolph said at the funeral got my attention," I said, "But it wasn't until I was on the phone with Campbell that I had the sudden thought that a guy accused of rape had a good motive to kill the one anteing up the dough to support his accuser."

"Interesting fact, don't you think, that this guy has a boat at the Northport marina?" Sam observed with irony.

"Damned interesting," Joan agreed. "It means he probably knew Fuss had a boat there too. That would incline him toward the 'fishing trip accident' setup."

"But is it likely that this Preskorn would go to Fuss's' house to kill him?" I was having trouble with that.

"Suppose Fuss heard the front doorbell ring and just closed the utility room door to keep Oscar there until he answered the door. Suppose It turned out that it was Preskorn, who hit Fuss on the head and killed him. Let's say he never knew about Oscar. Preskorn then took the body to the marina and tried to make it look like an accident. I'd say this guy is a serious candidate to be our murderer." Sam was smiling and nodding, pleased with his construction of events.

Coop spoke up. "Aunt Kirby, I read doubt in your expression."

"People generally run true to form and Blake Campbell said this man didn't have a history of outright violence. Fuss's killing was very violent."

"Anyone could be violent on an impulse," argued Sam.

"True. But was Fuss's murder on impulse?" she

countered. "There was much planning: the bogus breakfast, the bogus lunch and the inclusion of fishing tackle."

Sam conceded the point with a shrug, but it was plain to see he thought Preskorn was a hot suspect, and we were all wrong.

Coop decided to enter the debate. "Let's not dismiss him as a suspect just yet. After learning how Fuss was killed, we said we had to screen our suspects with three requirements in mind: means, opportunity and motive. When we learned the nature of the wound – a whack with a heavy object one inch wide - we decided anyone above the fourth grade could pass the test for means. Preskorn's opportunity is still to be determined – does he have an alibi? And while perhaps it's weak, he has a motive, since Fuss was supporting his accuser."

"OK, as a team, we'll keep open minds about Preskorn, but I know damn well that Vince tried to run over Al with his truck!"

No one argued wIth N.C. That would be wasted breath.

I'd called the meeting this evening to inform the group of how my call to Ben Reynolds had led to Blake Campbell and of the mind-blowing news N.C. and I had learned from him. Campbell's revelation about his partnership with Fuss was surprising to everyone, but no one believed the goal to name Fuss's murderer had been advanced much. Discouragement threatened. The reliable remedy for this condition in the past had been food. My new barbecue grill stood ready, so I began calling for burger orders. Rare and well-done were easy to satisfy, the ones in between were iffy. I got no easy orders this evening, but there were also no complaints.

While eating, I remembered and told the others of Campbell's parting speculation that Fuss's interest in helping young women might point to something in his past and wondered further if it involved Carla. "He suggested we talk to her."

"How do you begin that conversation?" Sam asked. "It would be something she'd rather forget and certainly not have people talking about."

"Maybe you could talk to her, Joan – or Kirby. Wouldn't she find it easier to talk to another woman?" I suggested.

"I'm sure she would," agreed Joan, "but even if it would be easier, I'd think she'd have no wish to talk to one of us about an experience like that."

"And what if her father's thing had nothing to do with her past?" Coop put forward. "That would be an awkward topic to bring into a conversation with her. 'By the way, Carla, have you ever been raped?'"

"C'mon Coop," I joked, "Since when have journalists been inhibited by poor taste?"

It was clear that no one wanted to pursue the issue with Carla, and it died right there.

About the time we finished the burgers, we also conceded the fact that now there were mosquitos and we moved inside for dessert.

Conversation was light. Topics were local and informative – who sold the best carry-out pizza etc.

The phone rang, and I answered. It was Jill, who explained she'd overheard our plan to meet at my house and was calling with some new information she'd just received and thought it would be important for the discussion we were having.

"My sister in Grand Rapids has a friend who's acquainted with Sharon Duval, the woman you saw Vince with at the restaurant. The friend thinks Sharon is planning to marry him soon."

"That is very relevant to our discussion, Jill. I'll tell the group right now. Thanks."

Reporting this to the gang furthered the conviction that Vince had killed Fuss to get half his wealth to run off with the new woman. This was followed by a chorus of "What gall" (Kirby), "That bastard" (N.C.), "Prick" (Coop), an unrepeatable blast from Sam and I thought I read "Creep" on Joan's lips.

As I watched the last person walk away toward their cars, I estimated where the investigation stood: Vince was our best suspect – we were waiting for Sheriff Davis.

# 17

Speculation the next morning at Caballo Bayo dealt with another important concern of ours - Jill's blossoming relationship with the young carpenter - a development threatening to rob us of her undivided attention.

"Jill can do better than that guy," Sam said in a dismissive tone.

"If only Jill had your taste, we'd have no problem," I observed.

Coop, who'd been the first to arrive had learned the guy's name was Adam. Coop also had been able to piece together the additional info that the young buck was going to be moving to North Carolina to join a cousin to start their own construction business. This was good news – right?

The trouble was, Jill seemed happy about his

plans. That didn't jibe with her evident pleasure with his coming to the café. This could have ominous portent. Worst case scenario? He'd asked her to go with him. After he'd left to go to his local job, and we received her smiling attention, none of us wanted to inquire further.

Conversation was desultory - Building was booming in the county and it was impossible to get someone to do a little job for you, like replace a window. Hops had seemed to be a winner crop for local farmers and turned out to be a complete flop, and so on. There was no attempt to expand the subject of Fuss's murder. Were we giving up? When we were breaking up and going separate ways, Sam came up to me.

"Al, this Preskorn guy was pretty much dismissed as a suspect last night, but I'm not so sure. It would be a mistake if we didn't check him out more fully. I've decided to go up to the Nothport marina and see what I can find out. How about coming with me?"

Firstly, his suggestion was reasonable, not promising, but reasonable. Secondly, I recognized Sam's need for support. Thirdly, I had no other plans for the morning and Kato had plenty of food in his bowl.

"Sure, why not."

I left my bike behind the Bayo and got into Sam's car. Closing the door, it occurred to me that this was a new experience. I had never been in a car alone with Sam, nor spent time alone with him in any way for that matter. When he wasn't at the Bayo he played golf – a lot. He belonged to the Leland Country Club where he played in the summer and a couple of clubs in Florida where he and Natalie had a condo. I had played only occasionally and then not well when I lived in Birmingham and here at Matheson Greens. When that course closed, I stashed my clubs in a corner of the garage and took up cycling.

"How are you hitting the ball, my friend?" Always a good way to begin a conversation with a golfer.

"In a rut. I used to have a 9 handicap . . ."

"Very nice."

"Yeah, but after my shoulder injury back in '94, I've been mired in the mid-nineties."

"I should have been so 'unlucky'."

Sam laughed. "I have hope though. I read an article in Golf Life magazine describing a new grip and a better backswing."

I said nothing to that, I didn't want to dampen his "hope." As I'm sure he knew, a suggested change of grip or swing is the core article of tons of issues of golf magazines in the past and would go on being so into the dim future. It occurred to me that a golf magazine must have a minuscule overhead – same article with a different author's name over and over again. Investing in one of these magazines would be an excellent source of retirement income.

"I hope it works out for you," I said. "Do you have friends in Florida that you usually play with?"

"Sure, although recently we've lost some guys – bad knees or hearts . . . or the worst."

"Does Natalie play?"

"Nah. She tried for a while and decided it wasn't her metier, as she put it. She believes a person should concentrate on what comes naturally - shopping in her case. Al, between you and me, when she dies, I'm having her stuffed as a mannaquin for Sak's window. She'd be in heaven."

Now here was a large topic. Sam had taken mild

kidding at the Bayo about Natalie's frequent excursions with her friends to the Meccas of fashion, but none of us, to my knowledge, had ventured beyond the surface. One never knows the absolute truth about the nature of other people's marriages. Most of us are willing to accept the version others want to present, so long as it works with our own lives. I'd bet Sam's marriage embraced a large compromise. Natalie was free to roam at large and shop with her friends - Sam could play golf as much as he desired – only if it was distant from his old Detroit buddies. What they'd worked out, I could never have lived with. It seemed to serve for them. Good. Leave it there. I needed another subject.

"Have you owned a boat, Sam?"

"I did for a while. Thought it would be good for business. Entertain customers, know what I mean? Got to be a big hassle – a pain. Invite one person, someone else is unhappy. Luckily Natalie got a little seasick once and I used that as an excuse to sell it. I still have my skipper's cap."

"I'll bet it looks good on you." I pictured him in my mind's eye all duded out in nautical gear. Laughing, I thought aloud, "Would it be good form to wear a skipper's cap on another skipper's boat?"

"You know, I'd never thought of that. That's one for Miss Manners for sure."

When we got to Northport, Sam drove to the waterfront and parked in the marina's main lot. There were plenty of people out on the different docks whom we could talk to – question about Lawton Preskorn. His name, however, was all we knew. It was pretty thin to go up and ask, "Do you know Lawton Preskorn?" I imagined the reply, "Who wants to know?"

175

"I wish you'd worn your skipper's cap."

Sam was not listening to me, not listening to the negative tone in my voice. He had for some reason really zeroed in on the playboy rapist as a good bet for Fuss's murderer. Hell, I hoped he was right. Time to get onboard with him I decided.

"Maybe our best place to start is the Harbor Master," I suggested. As it turned out, this saved us a lot of time.

"Good idea. Coop called him, Jim, I remember."

As we walked out to the office on the end of the first pier, I began putting together in my mind an inquiry that would be offhand, not one that would prompt caution on Jim's part. Wasted planning - Sam took charge.

Standing with Jim was a young man, who was of an age and demeanor that labeled him, "student- summer job." Jim had been leaning over the boy's shoulder pointing out some detail on a document lying on the desk. Sam marched in as Napoleon might have done commanding that you put aside your family and march with him into battle.

"Jim, maybe you remember me. My friends and I talked to you the day you discovered Fuss Quarrals's body. We need to know about a guy who has a boat here named Lawton Preskorn."

Jim looked up at Sam and blinked. As a matter of fact, he blinked four times before he was able to sort Sam's outburst into the heading of "inquiries about slip holders."

"I see," Jim said, "What is it you need to know?"

"We think he may have information that could help us understand how Fuss died."

Whew! I'd fully expected Sam to say, "He's the

one who killed Fuss!" That would, of course, have shifted Jim into caution mode. Good job, my friend.

"Yeah, well Lawton has a boat right on this dock." Jim turned and looked out the window back down the dock we'd just walked along. "Slip number 13. He has that Sabre 38 with the black hull."

I strained to think of what to ask next, when the question sprang to mind of its own accord. "Jim, do you record when a boat leaves the marina and returns?"

"No. Sometimes a person who is going out in the big lake wants me to know about it. That's usually only if there's a concern about the weather."

"So, to be specific, would you know if someone was out on their boat around the third and fourth of July – Lawton Preskorn for instance," Sam asked.

"Not usually, but in his case, I do know for sure."

Sam and I couldn't believe our ears. It's as if I'd asked my father for a quarter for the Saturday matinee and he'd handed me twenty dollars and said, "While you're at It, buy yourself a new first baseman's mitt."

Jim saw that we were struck dumb, so he explained, "There was this rowdy party on Preskorn's boat. It was on July fourth about noon, when other boat owners called me complaining, so I went down to talk to them.  One girl who hadn't been drinking, understood the problem and promised me she'd get help to restore sanity. That was her word, 'sanity'. I learned from her the party had started two days before in Harbor Springs, then had moved on to Charlevoix on the third before ending up here."

"Was Preskorn on the boat?" asked Sam.

"Yeah, I saw him."

I saw a possibility. "The girl said the boat and the

party traveled from Harbor Springs to Northport. That wouldn't necessarily mean Lawton Preskorn was with it. I mean, someone else could have operated the boat couldn't they have?"

Jim frowned, as if my question was far-fetched. "I don't get it?"

"I guess I mean that he could have been in Traverse City where he lives and only joined the party here."

Jim shrugged. "As far as someone else operating the boat – yeah, that's theoretically possible, but in real life, it's a no start. Preskorn wouldn't trust anyone to take the wheel of his boat. No way! I've heard people kid him about it."

There are times when a very complicated proposition you've been pondering has been categorically negated with a simple – no. Your mind is still cranked up ready for hours of debate making it difficult to accept that the case is closed. You can either accept and assimilate the truth or become . . . burdened. After a few seconds, I erased Lawton Preskorn from my mind. I glanced at Sam. For several moments, he looked up at the office ceiling rocking back and forth on the balls of his feet, then he said, "Win some lose some."

# 18

Sheriff Hoss Davis was back. He'd arrive today, he would be back in his office tomorrow, and Coop had made an appointment for us to see him the next afternoon. At our last meeting at my house two nights ago, we'd reviewed where we stood: (1) we were sure Fuss had been murdered, (2) Vince DeSalle was our prime suspect, (3) we had the evidence of the lunch and Oscar.

As we'd savored those first sips of coffee at Caballo Bayo this morning, the mood had been one of resignation with a pinch of hopefulness. We were resigned to our failure to accomplish our original, ambitious goal of catching the bastard who'd killed our friend. Our hope rested on the reputation of Sheriff Davis. He'd be the ally who'd finish the job.

Our table talk this morning involved the mode of

our presentation to Hoss Davis.

"We can't forget this Preskorn guy that Blake Campbell told us about," N.C. reminded the group.

"Oh yes we can," I asserted.

"Dead in the water," added Sam. "We'll tell you later."

"Good, that keeps it simple."

The plan we settled upon was this - Coop would turn out a captivating summary account of our efforts in a revisit to his Pulitzer Prize form. At the interview, we'd state our main claim – Fuss was murdered. Then, we'd hand Coop's write-up to Davis indicating that it set forth our thinking better than if the four of us tried to explain it there at the interview, probably repeating ourselves and muddying the water. We'd leave him knowing we were very serious and that we counted on him to consider our view just as seriously.

Jill had been very busy with the inside customers all morning, but when she brought us our checks, I briefed her on what we'd planned when we saw the sheriff.

"Whaddya think?" I asked.

"Hmm. Sounds . . . sterile."

Sterile? "Sterile?"

"I mean he just got back from this big trip with his wife to a far-off place he'd never been to before."

"Ah yes. You're right. 'Welcome back – hope you had a great time – hate to present you with something this serious so soon.' Like that, you mean?"

"Yeah, let him talk about the trip a little if he wants to."

"Right, right."

She smiled knowingly. I smiled back at her smile.

"Do you think you could get time off to go with us?"

She laughed. "No, no. The four of you are perfect."

This little lesson in empathy was on my mind when I left my friends. Although I'm sure when faced with Davis the recognition of and comment on his recent travel would have evolved naturally, the exchange with Jill put me in mind of another curtesy demanded in another relationship, mine and Carla's, or more accurately, what my relationship with Fuss demanded of me where Carla was concerned. I knew that her husband was having an affair. I knew Vince was planning to leave her. Regardless of what it would do to her feelings about me, I owed it to Fuss to tell her, and I couldn't put it off. Of course, I'd need to talk to her alone. I decided to drive the short distance to Fuss's house on the chance she might be there since the house was going on the market.

I didn't know Carla's car. It might be one of the three I found parked In Fuss's drlveway. If she were there, it was clear she wasn't alone. What the hell – I was here – I was curious – I got out and walked to the open front door.

One couldn't miss the bright green tags. One was attached to each of the living room pieces, even the throw cushions. Two women were in the dining room, standing back from the table fixing it with their attention. One woman held a laptop, making entries. The other gestured toward the table nodding her head. I walked toward them a few steps before the gesticulator noticed me and gave me the version of smiling face which meant "You're interrupting us, but what do you want?"

Confronting me were strangers treating my lost friend's cherished possessions as mere objects. This stirred the rebel in me to come up with a witty remark to tell them off. Some reasonable neurons must have vetoed that and reminded me I had other business.

"I'm looking for Mrs. DeSalle."

"She's in that room off the hall, the study," she answered brightly, relieved that disposing of me had been so easy.

At the study door my first impression was of the absence of green tags. Carla was sitting on a built-in bench in front of the window with an album in her lap. Reflexively, I glanced toward the bookshelf where I'd pushed what I'd thought to be a photo album back into the compulsive alignment of the other books. There was an empty space there now. At that same moment Carla looked up.

"Al, good to see you. Come and sit here. I think you'd be interested in these pictures of my father before you knew him."

"Yes, I'd like that."

She turned the pages back to the usual photos of a mother holding a new-born, a toddler learning to toddle, a boy riding a donkey, a cub scout giving the two-finger salute to the camera, progressing to an early teen standing next to a suitcase. It was only in the last picture that I could fully recognize the Fuss I knew. Carla lifted the edge of the next page. At its top, the place for the first photo was empty. The four paper corners pasted on to hold a picture were there, however. The next picture was of his sister's wedding. Both bride and groom exuded the spirit of endless optimism. Fuss looked to be in his early twenties and wasn't tuned to the same channel. I became vaguely aware of feeling dissatisfied as we looked at this picture.

My thoughts had turned to wondering about that sense of there being something missing when Carla, probably affected by the picture of her aunt's wedding, looked at me and made a sudden announcement.

"Al, it will be known by everyone soon, but I want you to know that Vince and I are getting divorced. We've discussed this for a long time. We've never been . . . compatible. We've delayed because of the kids. They're gone now. What decided it for us was Vince's meeting another woman and falling in love. Sharon. I've met her and I think it could work for them."

So, Carla knew. I immediately thought of what this meant for Vince being our main murder suspect. I couldn't listen to Carla politely and think about this. Did Vince still have the motive for murder? The question would have to wait until later. Also, I had to get my mind back on the album. The album. Yes, something bothered me about Fuss's pictures. What was It?

Clearly Carla was waiting for a response to the big personal news she'd just shared.

"I'm very sorry to hear that, Carla." I paused a moment before saying, "To be honest, I'm more concerned about your happiness than Vince's. To be honest again, I've never liked Vince very much." I waited to see how she took that before I added, "I believe this will be a good move for you."

She smiled and nodded faintly.

After a moment, I drew her attention back to the album, pointing to the photo of Fuss standing next to a suitcase.

"There's a caption under this, but I can't read it."

The pages of the album were black with a few words written in badly faded white ink under the photos.

Carla squinted at the almost invisible script.

"I'm off to W . . . Wakefield, of course. That's where Dad went to high school."

"Away from home, you mean?"

"Yes, a boarding school."

"Your family lived in Grosse Pointe, right? Why did he go away?"

"My grandfather went to Wakefield and wanted Dad to go to his old school. Carry on tradition you know."

"Huh. So, Fuss was a 'Legacy'; isn't that the word?"

I stared at the book a moment before it came to me. "There are no pictures of this Wakefield."

Carla blinked surprise. "Yeah. Right."

She turned the pages back and forth a moment.

"It's missing. A page is missing. I remember one snapshot in particular - Dad in his football uniform. He was so skinny and the shoulder pads looked so huge on him. And there were pictures with his roommate and other guys. And of the summer he was a camp counselor."

The album was a three-ring type, making the pages removable.

"What's that?" I said pointing to a ribbon of black paper deep in against the book's spine.

Carla teased it out with the tips of her nails and held it up. "Part of a page," she said.

We looked at the fragment a couple of seconds before I said the obvious. "That page was ripped out. This is the part that was left when the page was torn out and it dropped down near the spine of the album."

My eyes traveled to the top of the next page in the album. "And that picture was ripped from here too. See how these bottom two corner mounts are pulled up from the page."

Carla's face registered pure puzzlement.

"When was the last time you saw the pictures of your father in his football uniform?"

"Oh my God. Not since my kids were little and I was showing them the family pictures. But wait, I remember my daughter, Heather, showing these pictures to her fiancé only last month and they had a laugh at the shoulder pad picture."

"It's clear your dad wanted to remove this page from the album, and he must have been in a hurry. It would only take a few seconds more to open the rings and take the page out."

We looked up from the book into each other's eyes. "Can you think of any reason he'd need to do this in such a hurry?" I asked.

Clara shook her head. "No. It's so unlike something he'd do, and yet obviously he did do it."

I agreed. "Yes. Obviously."

"And this other picture here," I said pointing to the torn corner fasteners. "I'd say this photo was ripped out at the same time."

I added jokingly, "I can think of many of my adolescent snap shots that I would have wanted thrown out, but that was a long time ago. They no longer cause pain."

Carla was bewildered. She continued looking at the evidence of Fuss's hasty work.

Without my reading glasses, I couldn't make out

the writing under the missing picture. "Can you read what's written here?" I asked, pointing.

Carla leaned closer to the page. "'Me and  . . . Bucky', yes it says 'Bucky'."

We stared at the inscription for a moment and then Carla turned the page and continued showing me pictures of Fuss - one of several guys together on a porch holding up beer bottles apparently singing. I noticed a block "M" on a T-shirt.

"Fuss went to U of M, right?"

"Yes, that's where he met Mom."

"So, the missing page was of his time at the boarding school," I stated.

Carla didn't disagree.

Army pictures followed, leading up to Fuss's wedding.  He wore a first lieutenant's bar on the shoulder of his uniform.

Carla continued turning the pages tracing Fuss's young adult life. At first, my mind wanted to linger over the puzzle of the missing page, but I became absorbed in the progress of his family's life instead. Then it dawned on me that within that context I had my best opportunity to broach the question that had been my second reason for seeking her out today – to learn Fuss's motive for his legal support of young women. I took the chance.

"Carla, I believe you were as surprised as anyone to learn of your father's effort to provide a lawyer for young women who couldn't afford a lawyer on their own. Am I right?"

"Yes, it was news to me."

"Was your father's interest possibly motivated by something that had happened to you?"

There was no doubt my question surprised her. The surprise didn't arise from my asking a gauche question. It was a new idea to her.

"Ah . . . no. I can see why you might wonder, but no, it had nothing to do with any experience of mine.

So. So, another question had been answered that wouldn't advance our understanding of Fuss's murder - not even one space on the board. I got up.

"I'd better be on my way, Carla. You've got a lot to do here. It was wonderful of you to take the time to go through the album with me."

"It was my pleasure, Al."

"If there's anything I can do for you, just call. I know I also speak for the rest of the breakfast gang."

As I was turning, she said, "Just a moment, Al. Everything of Dad's that I want I've already set aside. Is there anything of his you'd like as a memento?"

"Fuss had a neat letter opener. If it's still available, I'd love to have it to remember him by."

Carla laid the album aside and went to Fuss's desk where she picked up the carved letter opener and handed it to me.

We parted with a hug.

Back in my car I needed to pause and go over all that had happened. Thirty years ago, I would have been able to perceive with all senses, evaluate relevance, assign value and organize response on the fly. Today, I must treat those functions separately and hopefully end up at the same point. What had I sensed? Carla did not seem to be stressed beyond what you'd expect to see in someone who'd recently lost her father and was breaking up her marriage. A load, yes, but she seemed in control. Maybe a future without Vince lightened that load. I could see that Vince still had the motive for Fuss to die before a divorce. That was still on the table. What else had I learned? Carla had not been the reason for Fuss's legal largess. I guess that whole business was a dead end. Of no value to us. What else? Yes, that crazy urgency of his to tear a page out of the family album. Again, one of history's lost answers. My thoughts here digressed, as they often do, into wondering how much of what we know of a person's history is merely that which did not die with them. Fifty percent? Thirty?

I studied the memento I held in my hand. The carving was intricate. I'd research it. Discover where in the world this kind of work is done. I'd Google it. So easy now. How much longer would it have taken me to get an answer about the letter opener's origin in the good old days?

I enjoyed the rest of the day at home puttering around outside just for a change, Kato always seeming to find something that needed to be examined in the vicinity. I returned a casserole dish to Susie Springer taking time for a short chat. Dinner today was one of my favorites, Colatura di Alici (spaghetti with oil, garlic and anchovy sauce.) Once the water comes to a boil, ten minutes until the first forkful. I took my second glass of zinfandel to my easy-chair and rifled through the news on my pad. Why do I do this? Reviewing the news was like a medieval monk wearing a hairshirt. I then watched an episode of "Slow Horses." The action moves too fast, or they talk too fast or both for me to know what's totally happening, but Jackson Lamb seems to know what's going on and our side will be the smart one in the end.

After a shower I went to bed, Kato curling up as

usual by my feet.  My constant routine was a couple of chapters of a mystery novel and then douse the light. In the middle of the night, I awakened with a jolt, opened my eyes wide and said aloud, "Who the Hell is Bucky?"

Kato raised his head and looked at me and then we both fell back asleep.

I remembered the dream in the morning - briefly - like most of my dreams.

# 19

I made the run to Caballo Bayo on my bike. It went well - no residual from the fall, "Good Boy" was pleased that I was back on the road. My three friends were already stirring their coffee with big smiles and greeted me with heartier than normal, "Good mornings." The reason, I was soon to learn, was because Biggs had offered the Carolina cousin of Jill's new heart throb a job here with his company, a job the young guy couldn't refuse. Jill would not be leaving us.

It was clear no one wanted to revisit Fuss's murder. The subject was shelved until our appointment with Sheriff Davis tomorrow. Instead, the subject was the universal one.

"Possible rain tomorrow," stated Sam. It was said in a manner of a remark on something we already knew, like, "You'll be older tomorrow."

"We should meet anyway to hear what Coop has written," I said.

"Right. Be on the same page when we see Davis," N.C. added.

A smiling Jill came by and filled cups. N.C. added sugar to his and began stirring.

"Would you return my spoon when you're finished there," Sam said, smiling and holding out his hand.

N.C. was nonplussed for a moment, replied, "I'll lend you *my* spoon, but it isn't yours."

"Sure it is. You picked it up off the counter," Sam insisted, pointing to the alleged spot where the disputed spoon belonged. "Who else could have taken it?"

N.C. looked around his place at the counter to be sure he didn't in fact have two spoons and having satisfied himself announced to all of us, "Sam has become delusional. Paranoid delusions. This morning it's a stolen spoon; who knows what he'll say tomorrow when we see the sheriff?"

Sam pleaded his case to Coop and me, gesturing to the spoon-less counter surrounding his coffee cup. "I repeat, who else could have taken it?"

Itch lumbered to his feet, causing N.C. to say, "Not yet old buddy. Not time to go home yet."

But Itch wasn't heading home. He had walked slowly to Sam's stool where he was investigating the shiny object that lay there on the ground.

We all stared at the errant spoon.

"And thus have many innocents been sent to the gallows," observed Coop in a solemn tone.

Laughing, Sam asked Jill for a clean spoon. "Itch stole mine," he explained.

"Reminds me of when I was a kid," began N.C.

"Ten or eleven."

"Is this a tall Cajun tale involving allegators?" I moaned.

"No. This was true and very serious. Hell, it liked to be crucially formative for me."

"Tell on. my friend," said Coop.

N.C put both elbows on the counter, holding his cup with both hands. His voice took on that quality of the storyteller. "Both of my folks were heavy smokers – Chesterfield. We weren't dirt poor, but there must not have been any money left over at the end of the week. Every penny had significance. What I'm getting at is the money spent on cigarettes must have accounted for a large slice of the pie. So, you can understand they'd notice when one or two cigarettes from their packs went missing each week. Where did they go? There were only the two of them, my three-year-old sister and me in the house. There were several boys whom I played with, some older than me. The answer was a slam dunk. Little N.C. was stealing the cigarettes, either to give to his older friends, or to smoke them himself, or both.

"It wasn't me. I'd never even thought of taking the damn things. The more I denied it the more of a hardened criminal I appeared to be. My parents consulted relatives and friends, who had remedies that varied from bribing me with candy to locking me outside at night with the gators. Today, I would be sent to a child psychologist. Back then it would have been a 'no starter' – no money and how do you spell 'sycoligist?' Of course, I wasn't allowed to play with my evil friends. This went on a long time. How can you remember just how long – time gets so distorted. Today's month seemed to be a year back then.

"One solution would have been to put the cigarettes where I couldn't get them. Lock them up! My father nixed that recourse. It would be a bad life-lesson if others were forced to accommodate to my pathology.

"I was advised to confess. I was told I was being punished more for my persistent lying than for my thievery. Now here's the thing. If a kid caves in and passively confesses to something he didn't do, a large cavity is hollowed out of his character. Instead, if he resists and elects to take the belt, he holds on to his whole self and instead sees that it's the adult world that's nuts. My many years now as an adult have done nothing to contradict that early insight.

"Anyway, during her spring cleaning, my mother included my little sister's doll house. She found it was stuffed with cigarettes. Sis had taken them for her doll tea parties for when the 'doll mothers' visited.

"And did my parents drop to their knees begging my forgiveness for their stupidity? No! You know they wouldn't have. It was an 'understandable mistake' - just like all our wars have been. And they were right: it was an understandable mistake when you accept the fact that the human brain is just doing its flawed best."

N.C. was laughing as he said this, so we did too. I began to applaud, and the others joined in.

"N.C.," I said, "That story needs to be included among Aesop's Fables."

Coop summarized. "Two lessons this morning on the need to beware of 'The Obvious.' Obviously, N.C. had taken Sam's spoon and N.C. had obviously stolen his parent's cigarettes."

"And *obviously* a carpenter named, Adam, must be inside, or Jill would have been here with our breakfast by now. Right? Wrong. I can see her talking to some girlfriends at one of the tables."

Jill came with our usual orders. We joked around in our usual way and left anticipating an usual day. Mine turned out to veer unusually toward the left. The bike ride home was pleasant. My thoughts were of my family whom I hadn't seen since Easter vacation. Someone in each my daughter's and son's family worked at jobs that only got government authorized time off. That meant it wouldn't be until Labor Day that I could look forward to getting them all together up here. It's a shame to leave this area in the summer – something like taking time off from the Riviera in the winter to visit Detroit – but I needed to make the drive to Chicago to see them all for a few days.

Approaching home, I noticed the mail delivery car pulling away from my box. I stopped and retrieved the half-dozen or so envelopes, most of which I knew would be requests for money.

I greeted Kato, checked his food and water and took the mail to my easy chair to open. Then, I remembered my new letter opener. I got it from the kitchen table where I'd dropped it when I'd come home with it from Fuss's house. Back in my chair I took a moment to study the carving again before I used it to open the first envelope on which was printed the picture of a bear. Obviously, they wanted money to save the endangered bear population. I withdrew the enclosed letter to find that it advertised "Bear Bros. Construction," who wanted to build whatever I desired to build. I chuckled aloud. Another "Obviously" gone wrong.

It was, at that moment, as if a mental tuning fork had been struck inside my head. Where else had

I recently heard, "obviously?" Maybe I remembered it because I was holding the letter opener which Carla had so recently held and handed to me. Yes, it was Carla who'd said it! She said, "It was so unlike something he'd do, yet *obviously* he did do it." Obviously Fuss had torn out the page from the album.

Superimposed in my mind was the lesson of the morning emphasized by Coop: "Beware of the word, 'Obvious'." N.C. obviously took Sam's spoon - He didn't. N.C. had obviously stolen the cigarettes – He hadn't. My letter obviously would ask money for an endangered species – It didn't. Jill was obviously talking to her boy-friend – She wasn't. Fuss obviously tore the page from the album – He didn't? . . . Someone did.

You tear a page out of an album, because you don't want people to see the pictures on that page. There were plenty of pictures of Fuss on other pages, so why that page? Then why not take that picture alone just as the photo had been taken from the following page? The answer must be that there were more photos on that page that had to be kept from viewing. It didn't make complete sense to me.

But wait, if Fuss didn't do it who did? I remembered then that there *was* one person whose name we knew whose picture *had* been ripped out of the book – "Bucky." "Me and Bucky." The Bucky who had made it into my dreams. I could call Carla and ask her who this person was. It was simple. Wait a minute! So what? Why was I getting involved with this. It was no business of mine. Carla would think the same.

I needed to take a break. Get back into my own life.

I thought of the bird/squirrel feeder I planned to

build and got up and began getting the wood and tools together.

I stopped and laughed at myself. My mind was only half on the project. The other half stood looking at the unanswered question – who is Bucky? I went back to the kitchen where I'd left my phone, looked up Carla's number and dialed.

Reading her caller ID, Carla answered brightly, "Hi, Al."

"Sorry to bother you with my silliness, Carla, but ever since we read the caption that read, 'Me and Bucky', where that photo had been torn out of your photo album, my mind keeps asking me, 'Who is Bucky?'. Please put me out of my misery and tell me who the guy is."

"Al, I'd be happy to, but I don't have any idea who he is. I'd guess he was one of Dad's friends. It seems they all had nicknames back then."

"No Idea at all?"

"No, it was never of interest to me. I listened more to my mom's stories than his."

"Thanks Carla, I'm sorry I bothered you."

"No bother. Sorry I couldn't help.'

There, that put a nail in it. Bucky could go to hell. I'd get back to feeding the fauna.

I was mounting a platform on the outside of the house under the kitchen window. I'd be able to replenish the seed from inside and watch the action while cooking. Both birds and squirrels could reach it, but Kato couldn't scale the flat wall to select a tender sparrow or titmouse for lunch. The squirrels would eat more than their share, of course, making this method a relatively expensive bird feeder. I was copying my friends Tim and

Betty, who had done this. They have contented smiles and probably sleep well.

I was up on the ladder when the phone rang. Fortunately. I'd stuck my phone in my pocket after calling Carla. I was surprised to hear her voice.

"Al, it just occurred to me that there may be someone who knows who Bucky is. Bradley Shields was a good friend of Dad's in high school and college. They've always kept in touch - Christmas cards and so on. He and his wife live in Arizona. They didn't come to the funeral – I think she's chronically ill – but they sent flowers."

I don't think well standing on ladders. So, very slowly I realized she was explaining that although she didn't know Fuss's high school friends, there was someone who did. A living guy with a current address.

"Oh, OK . . . great."

She said the guy's name and started to give me the phone number.

"Wait Carla! I've got to write this down."

"Just record it on your phone."

"You can do that?"

"You have a Voice Memos app. haven't you?"

"No, no. Just let me concentrate on coming off this ladder, one step at a time, then I'll get paper and pen and call you back."

I'm sure she was as bewildered with my response as I'd been with hers, but she said, "OK," and hung up.

My hunt for Bucky was still alive. This curiosity of mine had as much importance, however, as your obsessed search for the name of the actor who played the villain in a film you'd seen ten years ago. I found a pen and paper and called Carla.

"I'm ready," I said.

"His name is Bradley Shields. His number is . . . ", and she proceeded to give me that and the wife's name. "Oh, and it's Scottsdale."

"Thanks Carla. I'll call you and tell you if I've had luck – if you're interested."

"Sure, do that."

I judged that her interest equaled less than the weight of a postage stamp, but she was the kind of person who was ready to help anyway.

I had been in the middle of my critter feeding project and I hated to leave jobs partially done. On the other hand, here I was with my phone still in my hand. I dialed.

The voice that answered was forthcoming and friendly, as in "Hi friend, what can I do for you?" although all he'd really said was, "Hello."

I introduced myself as a former friend of Fuss's and we said a bit about how he'd be missed.

"I understand from his daughter, Carla, that you knew Fuss pretty well – Is that what you called him, or was it something else back then?"

"It was Fuss. He'd picked it up when he was a toddler as I remember."

"He was 'Fuss' as long as you knew him then?"

"Right. Of, course, I met him for the first time at Wakefield."

"That was your high school, the boarding school?"

"That's right, only people called it a prep school."

"Oh, right."

I don't know why I said, "Oh, right." The man I'd known, and my image of a "preppie" were far apart. Prejudice for sure, because I hadn't known anyone who attended a 'prep school.'

"Were you close to Fuss – like roommates?"

"There were four of us who hung out together pretty much through all those years, but no, I wasn't his roommate. I don't remember who he roomed with the first two years but in the junior and senior year he and Bucky roomed together."

Good God, there it was being handed to me like a gift.

"Bucky was a nickname I take it."

"Right"

He continued with the real name, and something else regarding Fuss, but I wasn't listening anymore. Then I tuned back to what he was saying and interrupted.

"Where is this school located anyway?"

"Wakefield? Why, it's in Newport, Rhode Island."

Shields continued talking about how he'd come to U of M and he and Fuss belonged to the same fraternity."

There were several seconds where neither of us had anything to say before he began telling me about the last time he'd seen Fuss. Fuss had visited in Arizona. I made the polite rejoinders, but my thoughts were elsewhere. "Rhode Island." Where had I heard that?

After thanking him for the information, I hung up and sat for a long time. Kato began rubbing my leg and I realized it had gotten to be time for his evening meal. I opened a can of his food and dished out a portion, then went outside, folded the ladder and collected my tools. I came inside and called N.C. to tell him I wouldn't be at Caballo Bayo for breakfast tomorrow.

"Oh," he said. "No problem I hope."

"You can tell the others . . ." I said, looking down at Kato's now empty bowl, "that Kato is not eating well and I'm taking him to the vet in the morning."

Then I called Beth Parker's number in Boston, who was clearly surprised by my call. After brief polite inquiries, I told her I had heard from Carole about her MeToo claim and asked if she could describe the boys who'd raped her.

She said nothing for a moment. The question clearly surprised her. Then I nheard her sigh.

"I've thought about them a lot as you might imagine. They were my age I believe. Their manner was different than the boys from my school - superior . . . entitled. It had been too dark to see their faces."

She went on about some other evidence to do with semen and panties that she'd now turned over to the police, but my mind was on another track.

I interrupted. "Was Wakefield Academy nearby?"

"Wakefield? Yes, it was."

I explained that something had come up that had got me thinking and I'd call her back to explain more fully. I thanked her and hung up. After that, I sat and thought until very late.

# 20

I'd had a very full morning. It was now ten o'clock. I'd had no idea when I awoke I'd be standing here now. There hadn't been time to think of what I'd say or do. I'd glibly talked myself into this moment and it was too late now to turn back. I raised my hand and pressed the doorbell.

Sam opened the door, surprised, but smiling.

"Al, c'mon in."

I walked to the center of the large living room as Sam closed the front door.

"Sorry to hear Kato is under the weather. What did the vet have to say?"

"Kato's good . . . Bucky."

He was clearly gobsmacked, but only for a micro-moment. His comfortable smile again settled in place.

"I haven't heard that for years – my nickname

back when I was a kid. How did that come up?"

I was sure he hadn't wanted to ask that, but it would have been very strange in normal circumstances if he hadn't.

"Bradley Shields told me."

"Shields? 'Sticks' Shields? That was his nickname. He had a cast on his leg for a while and walked with crutches. How did. . . Oh, of course. Fuss's funeral. Did he come here later?"

Sam was just rambling, trying to find a soft spot to land.

"No. He couldn't make the funeral trip; his wife was ill. No, I called Shields to see if he could tell me who 'Bucky' was."

He wasn't going to ask another question. He was waiting to see where I was headed.

"You can imagine my surprise to find out that you and Fuss had been classmates. Why hadn't you ever said so? Very strange that. All those times we were together and no mention of this significant fact about your longstanding relationship with Fuss."

I paused to see if he would respond. He just stared at me.

"I stopped by Fuss's house yesterday hoping to see Carla without Vince around. I felt I needed to warn her about Vince's plans to leave her. She was there. The estate sale people were putting price tags on the furniture. I found her in Fuss's study looking over the family photo album and she invited me to join her. She wanted to show me Fuss's childhood pictures. It was a typical ringed notebook type of album, pictures secured to the pages with glued-on corners. The last picture on one leaf showed Fuss standing next to his suitcase.

A caption under it read 'Off to Wakefield'. Carla said it was a boarding school. Then we discovered that the next page had been torn from the book. A piece of the absent page remained down near the spine. Also, the first picture on the following page had been torn out. Beneath it was a caption written in faded white ink – 'Me and Bucky'. The missing page had been of the time when Fuss was at the boarding school. Carla didn't know many of Fuss's school friends and thus didn't know who Bucky was. She said Bradley Shields probably remembered since he and Fuss had been classmates. There's your answer, Bucky."

Again, I discerned that he didn't know what to say. Finally, he pointed to a chair and said, "Why don't you sit down, Al."

I did, and since he wasn't going to ask the question, I asked it for him.

"You're probably wondering why I was so curious about the identity of this 'Bucky' in Fuss's family album."

Yeah, he was wondering alright, and while I was sure he didn't really want to pursue the question, he nodded.

"You see, the way it looked to Carla and me was that Fuss had torn a page from the book and he'd done it urgently, because he hadn't simply opened the rings and taken out the page, he ripped it out leaving behind that remnant of the page. Also, the single picture appeared to have been ripped off the next page. Why would Fuss, who was so meticulous about everything he did, do this? It looked as if he had suddenly wanted to remove evidence of his having been at this school - Wakefield. The pictures, Carla remembered had been in the album a short time ago. Why do this now? I had many questions when I left Carla's, but they were idle questions that only related to Fuss's strange behavior. It wasn't until later yesterday, when considering some other facts that I said to myself, 'Maybe Fuss didn't tear out the page. Maybe someone else did: someone who may also have been in those pictures. Who could that be?' I had only one name – Bucky."

Sam laughed. "Well, it wasn't me. I didn't know he even had an album."

I nodded. "You can follow my thinking though. One - It was done recently as Carla affirmed. Two - Fuss didn't do it, not like him. Three – Who had made changes in Fuss's house recently that we know of? Answer - the person who killed him and put out the fake breakfast dishes. Four – So, maybe another change the killer thought he needed to make was to take his pictures out of Fuss's album. Why? So, there would be no proof that he knew Fuss back in prep school. Why again? Are you with me so far?"

"No, not really. You went through that too fast for me to check your logic." He laughed again. "I have the notion that if I agreed with each step of your argument, you'd end up proving I'm the King of Siam."

I smiled. "I wish that were true." I looked at him steadily then for a few seconds before continuing. "Let me tell you about something I learned from Bradley Shields that corrected a small bit of misinformation that allowed me to understand everything . . . well not everything. I need your help with some of the details."

Sam did not like this whole scene. I saw that his discomfort was mounting.

"I've been too vague; I'm sorry. OK, the hard facts. Back in the early summer of the year you graduated from Wakefield, Beth Parker, our former UN Ambassador, was raped by two young men about her age, who talked and behaved differently than the boys she was used to being with. They were, to use her words, 'superior and entitled'. She wondered if they were from one of the two prep schools in the area – Newport, Rhode Island.

The police never pursued her claim, saying it was too late for a physical exam and the schools had already dismissed the students at the year's end. A while ago, Beth Parker joined the MeToo trend to publicly reveal that she had been raped back then. Knowing that my friend Carole Stuart had been Beth Parker's college roommate, I asked Carole if she knew about the rape. She did. Beth had described the rape to her in detail. When I was on the phone with Bradley Shields I learned that Wakefield Academy is in Newport - Newport, where Beth Parker was raped by two boys, who were possibly from one of the prep schools. When I heard 'Newport', alarms went off big time."

I paused. If I were badly wrong Sam's expression should be one of complete bewilderment right now. It wasn't. It was one of acute anxiety.

I continued, "Another fact that our group had been puzzled about was Fuss's funding the legal support of young women who claimed they had been sexually assaulted. Why did he do this? Had Carla been a victim? I asked her. She denied it. So why then? Suddenly, BONG! It came to my mind. It was because, he had been one of the boys who had raped Beth Parker and he felt guilty. Who was the other boy? You, of course, Sam."

"Bull shit! That's pure bullshit. How can you sit

there and fucking say that?"

He was obliged, of course, to react. He stood up and pointed to the front door.

"I should throw you out, you bastard."

Should throw you out, he'd said. He should be wondering if he dared to let me go.

"Keep your shirt on, Sam. This part about the rape is not speculation; it is all but proven. I called Beth Parker last night to ask her what she remembered of the guys who'd raped her. She told me that while the police hadn't done a post-rape physical on her, she had saved the semen smeared panties she'd worn that day. At first, she kept them out of anger, but later when she learned of DNA matching, she knew she held the identity of the rapist. She told me she's now turned this evidence over to the police."

That should shake his confidence!

Sam stood blinking – confounded. In a faltering voice he asked, "Did you tell her your suspicions about Fuss and me?"

"No, I didn't. I wanted to talk to you first. And anyway, that first crime is not my real interest. What I need your help with, Sam, is the second crime. The crime our group has been trying to solve – Fuss's murder. I understand this much; that you, 'Bucky', thought you needed to disassociate yourself from being a classmate of Fuss's at Wakefield. More precisely, you wanted to erase your friendship with him at the time of the rape. Now I puzzled over why this had become such a hot issue for you after all these years. I don't know the answer, but knowing Fuss as I did, I have a hunch. Here's what I think. Beth was coming here on the Fourth. I'll bet an extension of the same guilt that had Fuss hiring lawyers for young women propelled him into wanting to make his own public confession of his crime while she was here in Leland. Am I right"

Sam looked frightened.

"Sam, I think you *planned* to kill Fuss to prevent him from making a public confession."

"NO!" he shouted. Then quietly he said, "That's not the way it was."

Thank God! This is what I needed!

"Then, tell me about it, Sam."

He first looked down long enough that I thought he wouldn't go on, but then he looked up at me.

"It was just like you said. The damned fool got this crazy idea that he needed to confess. 'I've got to clear my conscience before I die and her coming here is a sign,' was the way he was carrying on. I tried to get him to see that doing so was going to hurt a lot of people we both cared about; Carla, his grandchildren, his friends, Natalie and my friends and it wouldn't change what had happened in the past. He was deaf to whatever I said."

Sam stopped and looked down at the floor and shook his head.

"He was on his knees fixing a leak in the utility room sink and I was pleading with him to listen to reason. He finished his job and handed the wrench to me, so he could use both hands on the sink to help himself up. He was being so damned stubborn. I just lost it for an instant and bopped him on the head. I was shocked by what I'd done and tried to help him up . . . finally, I realized he was dead."

He looked at me, willing me to understand.

"I never meant to hurt him. Shit, I was at my wits

end." He was silent for a long moment then continued' "You know the rest. I tried to make it look like he went fishing. Crazy idea . . . made some mistakes – leaving Oscar – I didn't think of the fake lunch until I saw his cooler in the Jeep. I didn't want to go back to his house to make the sandwich so I stopped at home and made it. Wrong stuff! – I did think to stick my bike in the back of the Jeep to get home from the marina. My adrenalin must have been pumping or I'd never have been able to carry him all the way from the Jeep to his boat."

"And you went further than you should have by tearing that page out of the album," I added. "You and Fuss must have agreed that you should bury those years when you were together at Wakefield Academy in order to sever any association with Beth Parker's rape. You knew of those pictures in Fuss's family album and you were afraid you'd be recognized. But, by tearing out the pictures, you actually drew attention to them."

Sam looked completely defeated.

"I understand how you felt, Sam. Fuss could be a frustrating, stubborn ass. Further, I think you were right; a lot of people would have been hurt with nothing of equal value gained."

Hope showed on his face. I seemed to understand.

"However," I went on, "You took Fuss's life. Sparing someone's feelings or your own reputation never justifies murder."

Throughout this last bit of explanation, Sam had gotten up and had been slowly moving toward the side of the room near the front window. He opened a drawer in a desk there and withdrew a revolver. Sam had a gun? He was always outspoken for banning hand guns!

I'd made a big mistake.

"I can't let you leave here, Al," He said soberly. "All I've been through would be worthless, if you were free to talk. I'm sorry, but it's really the same argument I made to Fuss. Nothing to be gained, only other people getting hurt."

I had been working toward getting him to confess, but I hadn't worked out a script for this scenario.

"WAIT! Sam," I choked out desperately. "You need to see this first."

His action had been interrupted.

I began fumbling to unbutton my shirt, then I just ripped it open.

"I'm wearing 'a wire,'" I gasped.

Taped to my sternum was a small metal object, a microphone and whatever chips were necessary to send a signal - not the impressive gadget and wires displayed in an episode of *Dragnet*. I hoped it was convincing enough.

"Sheriff Davis and his men have been sitting out there on the road listening to all we've said here."

Sam looked out his front window. Coming quickly toward his door was a giant of a man flanked by several others heavily armed and wearing tactical gear. Sam put the gun back in the drawer and closed it. He turned and began walking toward the door.

"Excuse me, Al. I believe we have visitors."

# 21

As soon as the radio-device had been removed from my chest, I left Sam's house. I didn't want to be there throughout the procedures dealing with his arrest, handcuffing and transport to jail. I got in my car, then had to stop to take several deep breaths to calm myself before I started the engine. That last half-hour had been more stressful than I could have imagined. I desperately needed the company of a friend. I made a dash to N.C.'s place.

Itch, lying on the front porch, made the effort to stand and wait for the expected pat on the head. N.C. having heard my car drive in, opened the screen door.

"How's Kato? Did he really have a problem?"

"Kato's fine, but I'm in immediate need of a beer and CPR!"

He frowned. "What's wrong?"

"Get those beers and come back to the porch and sit down here. You don't want to hear what I have to say standing up."

He returned with two cans, turning an empty rocker to face me.

"I've just come from Sam's house where Sheriff Davis arrested Sam for Fuss's murder."

The words I'd spoken still shocked me. N.C stared at me for several seconds.

"Say What?"

"Sam killed Fuss. But it's going to take a while to explain how it came about."

I became aware then that I was rattled – shaking a little even – more than a little.

"Hell N.C., I'm more shaken by what just happened than I was admitting to myself. I need to sit here and sip this beer a minute."

As I tried to sit back and relax, Carla came to mind. The sheriff would be going out to her house to tell her the story, but I felt like she should hear it from me first. I took out my phone.

"N.C., you said the other day you had Carla's number in your phone. Please look it up for me."

He read the number off and as I dialed, I noticed him dialing another number and going into the house.

Carla answered and I said, "Carla this is Al. I have something to tell you that is going to upset you a lot. Before I do, I think you should sit down."

She didn't question that advice.

"I'm sitting, Al."

I described the scene in the utility room and how in a moment of anger Sam had hit and killed her father and then tried to cover it up. She reacted as I'd expected with disbelief and renewed grief.

"Carla, the sheriff will be there with you soon, but I wanted to be the one you heard this from first. I hope you understand."

I could hear her sobbing for several moments before she said brokenly, "Yes . . . thank you, Al."

I heard her hang up. From what I'd seen of Sheriff Davis, I was sure she would be in good hands. Who knows, maybe even Vince would come through for her. In addition to dealing with the idea of her father being murdered, she'd also have to come to terms with his part in the rape of Beth Parker.

N.C. returned to the porch with two more beers.

"I called Coop. He and Joan were at Kirby's. They're coming right over."

Good, I thought. This would give me half an hour or so to get my nervous system under control. This experience of "losing it" was an unusual one for me. I had always been the one who remained calm and focused, ready to concentrate on the next action to be taken. Another little surprise that aging had in store. Thank God I'd been in command of myself back there at Sam's. N.C. and I sipped beer and marked time until Coop, Joan and Kirby arrived, and everyone settled on the porch. Ruth announced she had coffee brewing. They looked to me now to tell the story.

"First, let me say that once I'd hit upon the idea of Sam being the killer, it was imperative that my suspicion not be known to Sam until I'd had a chance to talk to Sheriff Davis. So, I hope you understand why I didn't share my thoughts with all of you before I could see him."

I had no organized presentation of what had been

a mental trapeze act for me. I hoped I'd not leave them more confused than informed.

"Looking back," I began, "My chain of thinking that ended in my belief that Sam was guilty went back to N.C. mentioning that Beth Parker had made a MeToo claim.

Then I learned from Carole Stuart that the rapists had been two strange boys Beth thought to be her own age. She had graduated that week from high school in Newport, Rhode Island. In other words, boys from another Newport school."

"Next thing. I felt I owed it to Fuss to give Carla a heads-up that Vince was seriously cheating on her and at the same time I wanted to ask her if Fuss's legal support of young women could be related to any early experience of hers. I went to Fuss's house, where they were preparing for an estate sale. Turns out she already knew about Vince, and she'd had no early problems that would account for Fuss's legal charity. Carla was sitting in Fuss's study looking through the family photo album and invited me to join her - see her father as a boy."

I then described to my friends in detail how Carla's and my looking through the Quarrals' family photos led to my learning Fuss had gone to a boarding school. And then of how we discovered that a page had been torn from the album as well as a single picture from the following page with the faded caption, "Me and Bucky". The page and picture would have covered the time he had been at the boarding school. I emphasized to the group the very significant fact that Carla was sure the album had been intact only weeks before our viewing. That fact had confounded me. Why would Fuss, who did everything in such a neat and tidy fashion rip a page of pictures of himself at school out of the family album? It came to me the next day that not only were Fuss's pictures missing, but also this "Bucky's" picture was gone. Then a "light bulb" question came to mind – who did we know who had recently made other changes in Fuss's house, like the cereal bowl on the dining room table? Answer: Fuss's murderer! A call to another of Fuss's high school classmates furnished Bucky's real name – Sam August, and that their prep school was located in Newport, Rhode Island. Then another "light bulb" lit up. Two boys Beth Parker's age had raped her. Two boys she didn't know, meaning from another school. Fuss and Sam were from another school in Newport. Finally, Fuss's murder occurred when Beth Parker arrived in Leland for the Fourth of July holiday. Was that merely a coincidence or the trigger? My reasoning said, coincidence be damned! I took it to Sheriff Davis wanting support for my conclusion. I wanted support for my reasoning, but my heart, on the other hand wanted my reasoning to be nuts. I liked Sam a lot.

"Wow," said Kirby. "Complicated. But so speculative."

"That's what Davis said. He nodded all through my argument then said just that, 'You haven't got a shred of real evidence.' And understand he was already half-way on our side. That deputy, who was at Fuss's boat when I saw the phony lunch, didn't give the box to Vince after all, but saved it to show to Sheriff Davis when he returned. I'd gone there ready to argue against Payne's accident theory, but found Davis had already tossed that out in favor of murder.

"In desperation, I came up with the idea of wearing a 'wire'. I was at my wits end. Davis wouldn't even consider it. 'Out of the question' he said."

I laughed. "He was right. But, I kept saying I knew Sam well and knew he'd admit what he'd done when I confronted him. What bullshit that turned out to be. I was crazy to insist, and Davis was even crazier to finally agree.

"No way was Sam was going to admit what he'd done when I confronted him. He was like a mafia witness, he didn't know what I was talking about. I went through my reasoning, which I just explained to you and all the while he stone-walled it, until I accidentally happened to hit upon the right combination of words that he had to respond to. I said, 'You *planned* to kill Fuss to keep him from making a public confession.' It was the 'planned' that he couldn't swallow. That meant premeditation. He shouted, 'NO! That's not what happened.' He, of course, realized he had just confessed and went on to describe how he was trying to reason with Fuss while Fuss was on his knees in the utility room repairing the drain. Fuss handed him the wrench so he could use both hands to help himself get up. Sam said he was so mad at Fuss's stubbornness that he gave him a 'little bop' on the head. He was shocked to discover it had killed him.

"It never occurred to me that Sam owned a gun. He was for banning all hand guns and assault rifles. You know what I mean, you've all heard him. Well, he did have a gun! He took a revolver out of his desk and said he couldn't let me leave his house or all he'd done would have been for nothing. I screamed, "Wait!," and yanked open my shirt to show him the transmitter strapped to my chest."

I laughed. "It was a tiny device and I became

afraid the damn thing was too small to convince him. I babbled out that Sheriif Davis had been sitting outside in his car listening to everything we'd said. Sam looked out the front window and here came Davis and his deputies."

I stopped and looked around the group. They were transfixed.

Now came many questions. Kirby remembered that it had been Sam, at our first meeting, who'd been the one to suggest a 'set-up'.

"That's right," agreed Coop. "Our discussion had been heading in that direction, but he'd been the one to say it and it was effective. One tends to eliminate the person who first yells 'This is not an accident!'"

We paused, remembering that first meeting of ours.

N.C. then said, "It's such a surprise finding out Sam and Fuss knew each other earlier in their lives - were classmates in fact."

A general response of, "Right" and "Yeah" came from the others.

I replied, "I've had more time to speculate about this than the rest of you. What I concluded is after the rape they had intentionally gone their own ways until they happened to be reunited up here. They had been best friends in prep school and we've witnessed that they still liked each other. Clearly it became of maximum importance to distance themselves from the rape so that anything linking them with the rape had to be avoided at all cost. They decided that their past history with the school, with Newport, Rhode Island and with each other must be erased."

There was silence while everyone considered this.

"The rape was never forgotten by Fuss," observed Joan. "I'm talking about his support of the young women."

"That's the hardiest thing to hear - that they were rapists," said Kirby her voice reflecting her dismay.

"Very true," I agreed. "We'll hear more details about that when Sam is charged."

There was silence and nodding of heads.

I had already imagined a likely scenario. Graduation day, feeling special, freedom from a restricting regimen, a party, too many drinks, full of themselves, spotting a pretty "townie" in a secluded location, two egos untethered . . . then the mistake of a lifetime!

A heavy mood had decended on our little group. They'd had to cycle through strong emotions in a short time. As for myself, I suddenly felt very tired.

"Friends, my pertrol tank has run dry. I think I'll head home."

"Right on," urged N.C.. "You've had a hell'uva day."

Coop said, while getting up, "We'll stop by the Bayo and talk to Jill. She'll be dying to know the main facts."

After hugs all round, I drove home.

There were two calls I needed to make. Blake Campbell took my call immediately. I gave him the simple facts and we made a date to have coffee and talk further. Beth Parker should be told about the persons who raped her, but I elected to call Carole Stuart and give her the story. She and Beth were old friends. Better that way. Next Jeff Springer rang my doorbell. He brought cookies from Susi. I suspect he'd really come for information, having heard, like much of the county, about Sam's arrest.

Once Jeff had gone it was dinner - French toast and a couple of glasses of wine. Usually, Kato joins me in bed. Tonight, he was there first - feline advice?

BANG! Lightning flashed through the bedroom window. Rain hammered the roof. Summer thunder-storm. Get up.  Close window. Back to bed. Rain on window . . . washing away . . . washing away.

# 22

When I opened my eyes, I knew my world would be back on course as if I'd put my finger on a spinning globe and brought it to a standstill. There would be a permanent sadness: Sam was an apprehended murderer. Both friends revealed as rapists. But everything was clear now, where confusion had prevailed.

The morning was crystal clear and cool. The ride was effortless with a southerly breeze at my back. I pushed my bike up and leaned it against the tree at the side of the building. Both N.C. and Coop had arrived. Jill served the coffee. We kidded around, talking nonsense. A mixture of anger and sadness hung in the background like a tapestry. No one mentioned it. We were saturated. Later, of course, it would all be reviewed - and reviewed, but not now - not yet.

N.C. began telling of a time when he walked into his mobile field office back in Jefferson Parish only to find a huge rattlesnake coiled in front of his office chair. He'd called one of the other men over and asked, "What shall we do?" The guy said, "Whatever he wants us to do - He de man!"

I waited to see if Jill would take the old rascal's bait. She did.

"How did you get him out of there, N.C.?"

He leaned back, satisfaction in his voice.

"Well, young lady, I peeked in the doorway and said, 'Friend, I just heard something that I'd bet you'd want me to tell ya. Heard that your neighbor just went over to pay a call on your old lady.' BAM! He was outta there lickity split."

She laughed, shook her head knowing she'd been taken in, and walked away to prepare our breakfasts.

We were still waiting for her to return, when Coop drew our attention to a guy, who looked about our age, approaching Caballo Bayo with a golden retriever on a leash. Coop slipped off his stool and jogged a bit in the guy's direction, calling out, "If you're planning on having breakfast, we'd like you to join us."

The guy stopped, considered for a moment, smiled and then crossed the grass to the outside counter. We introduced ourselves. He was Lenny Klein, the dog was Fred. Fred and Itch savored each other's pheromones. The four of us awaited the verdict. Fred wagged his tail. Itch gave a friendly moan and settled back on the ground next to N.C.'s stool.

"This looks like a regular thing - early morning - eating outdoors," Lenny said motioning toward the plates Jill had just deposited.

"Every day weather permitting," I answered, inviting him toward one of the empty stools.

"Cool," said our new friend.

The End

Printed in the USA
CPSIA information can be obtained
at www.ICGtesting.com
LVHW091739161023
761251LV00003B/355

9 780979 852596